Train Wheels, Flying Saucers and the Ghost of Tiburcio Vasquez

G. Lloyd Helm

Credits

Cover Artist: Designs by Ms G
Editor: Sherry Derr-Wille

Printed in the United States of America

DEDICATION

Like all my other work, this book is dedicated to Michele who believed.

CONTENTS

TIBURCIO'S TREASURE

The Hole in the Wall bar was misnamed because there was no 'wall.' It was just a dry, brown, ghost town-looking shack so far out in Southern California's Antelope Valley, a desert valley where there have been *no* antelopes in living memory, that I was always amazed it even had running water and electric lights. The shack sorta stuck up out of the creosote bushes in the bottom of this low place that might have been a volcanic crater a couple billion years ago. You could see the lights of the place for miles if the night was moonless. There was only one road, unpaved, leading to it, and it was made out of dust so gritty-fine it could blast the chrome off a truck bumper with just the slightest encouragement of a breeze.

How and why *The Hole in the Wall* got to be such a gathering place I don't know, but it was. Some ways it reminded me of Callahan's Saloon from the Spider Robinson stories only without the intergalactic clientele, at least I don't think there were any space aliens, but after what happened, I'm not quite so sure. Aliens or not, it did manage to attract a pretty wide cross section of folks. One time when I was leaning on the bar, I looked around and saw two Hells Angels, a drunk-on-his-ass Air Force colonel, a couple of Goth chicks with purple hair and bad attitudes, a priest of dubious reputation, and a couple of old timers who might have been the ghosts of every donkey dragging prospector who had ever poked through the Tehachapi Mountains looking for gold. I even saw a bridal party come in there one night complete with fooffy-gowned bridesmaids and tuxedoed groomsmen. But the night I met the ghost of Tiburcio Vasquez, there was nobody in the place except me, my friend Big Dave Dodge, and the barkeep who called herself 'Rio Rita.'

Big Dave was a six foot six, two hundred seventy pound, longhaired, goateed, mean looking, chopper riding…poet. He was gentle as a new mother most of the time unless you got him really stirred up, which was not easy to do. If a fella did manage it, he would be well advised to hit the bricks running because Dave could pick up a motorcycle, okay a small one, and lift it above his head. You would have expected his poetry to be something right out of the Beats or maybe a kind of Gangsta Rap but it wasn't. It was classical verse Robert Frost would have been proud of. It didn't make him any money though, so he put his great talents to work writing the sloshyist garbage imaginable and selling it to greeting card companies. He wasn't getting rich, but between that and his gigs playing 'Outlaw Biker' movie extra roles, he was eating regular with enough left over to visit *The Hole in the Wall* once in a while.

Well anyhow, one late evening Dave and I were leaning on the bar sipping suds and talking when I said to Rita, "Your last name's Vasquez isn't it?"

"Yep," she answered.

"Any kin to Tiburcio Vasquez?" I thought I was joking. Vasquez isn't quite as common a name as Smith, Jones or Garcia but it is pretty common.

"Yep," she answered. "My great, great grandfather."

"Really?"

"Oh yeah. I been hearing stories about Grandpa Tiburcio since I was a kid."

"Okay, I'll bite," says Dave. "Who is Tiburcio Vasquez?"

"You live out here and you never heard of Tiburcio Vasquez, the most famous bandito in all the great Mojave?"

2

Dave shook his head.

"You want to tell him Rita, or me?"

She suddenly got this speculative look on her face that piqued my curiosity. She'd always piqued my curiosity. She was one of those Latino women who could be any age between eighteen and a hundred. Long black hair, obsidian black eyes and an aspect that at one look made her the most gorgeous creature alive, and at another a crone out of some spook story. After a moment, she said, "Go ahead."

"Okay, but you can stop me if I go wrong." She nodded and I continued. "Tiburcio was a Californio from an old family that went back to before California was a state. Him and a lot of Mexicans were more than a little upset when the Anglos came looking for gold in 1849 and didn't ever go away again. When the Anglos began making all the Californios into second class citizens it didn't make for a happy place. Tiburcio and several others got upset and started talking revolution to take California back from John C. Fremont and the boys, but they were pretty disorganized so they wound up mostly as gallows apples. That also happened to Tiburcio, but he had a pretty good run as a thieving, murdering bandito for quite a while. He was better at it than Joquin Murietta and Elfago Baca. Terrorized the borax mining companies and anyone else who ever set foot in the Mojave. From what I hear he didn't have any of Zorro anywhere about him. He robbed from rich and poor alike and kept it. Supposed to have left a stash of gold and stuff somewhere up here. People been looking for it since he got hung. "

Dave looked at Rita. "And he was your great grandpa?"

"Me and about hundred others. Tiburcio got around."

"A romantic, huh?" I said. "I didn't know that."

"Oh yeah. It was what got him hung really."

"Yeah? I didn't know that. Guess you should have told the story."

"You did pretty good for an Anglo, but Grandpa Tiburcio and his gang robbed and killed people from San Francisco to San Diego, not just in

3

the Mojave. Worse than that, he was a handsome devil that made all the ladies wet their panties. That's why I am hardly alone in my kinship to him." The speculative look came back to her face as she looked over us, as though she was trying to decide whether or not to tell us something else. We sipped beer for a little then she bent down and got a bottle of really good tequila out from under the bar and poured three shots. "Drink up and I'll tell you some more about my grandfather," she said, shoving a plate with lime wedges and a salt shaker on it toward us. All three of us did the 'lick it, slam it, suck it' with the tequila then Rita leaned in closer to us. "I got a part of my grandpa his other grand kids don't," she said.

"And what would that be?" Dave asked.

She looked around as though the walls might have ears, then pointed at a half gallon pickle jar sitting on a shelf above the back bar. I'd never noticed it there before. It contained something that looked kinda like a big mushroom with half the cap gone. "Reach that down for me," she commanded, so I walked around, got it down and put it on the bar beside the tequila bottle.

"What is it?" I asked.

"El Miembro Masculino de me abuelo Tiburcio."

My Spanish ain't great, but it didn't have to be to understand what she said. It was Tiburcio's—well, his generative organ, as they would have said in Victorian times.

"You mean that's his…" Dave said, looking a little pale under his road tan.

Rita nodded.

But my Momma didn't raise no fools that would believe just any old thing so I said, "Naw, that's gotta be a joke Rita! That can't be his…It's gotta be a mushroom or something."

Rita didn't take offence. She just lifted her left hand as though taking an oath and crossed herself with her right.

I picked up the jar and shook it a little. Dave got paler still and said, "Hey take it easy with that. You don't want to drop it or nothing."

I sloshed it again. "So if this is the old boy's pud, how did you get a hold of it, no pun intended? How did he lose it?"

"I told you. That," she nodded at the jar in my hand, "is what lead to Tiburcio getting hung. See, he had hundreds of girlfriends from San Francisco to Tijuana, but he got eyes for the wife of a cholo in his gang. He went after Rosaria Leiva and Abdon, her husband, couldn't take it, so he went to the sheriff and made a deal to betray Tiburcio for the eight thousand-dollar reward and amnesty for himself. Abdon lead the sheriff to Tiburcio's hideout over in Agua Dulce, and after a big gunfight, Tiburcio was captured. They took him to San Jose to try him, and while he was in jail more than a thousand women came to see him. Not just Mexican women either. High society Anglo ladies from San Jose and San Francisco came and brought gifts and gave money for his lawyers. If women'd had the vote and been able to sit on juries then, Tiburcio might not have gotten hanged, but he did. They say that all the women in San Jose cried when he died. But Abdon Leiva wasn't satisfied with just getting Tiburcio hung. He went and bribed the undertaker with the eight thousand dollars then he cut *that* off..."

Dave and I both winced.

"...and put it in a jar with a quart of tequila like the worm at the bottom of a mescal bottle. Then he took it home and gave it to Rosaria."

"Oh man! That's cold!" Dave said.

Rita nodded and continued. "Rosaria got even with him though. Waited till Abdon was asleep and killed him with an ax."

"Whoa! What happened to her?"

"She got caught and they hung her too."

Dave and I looked at each other when she fell silent, then he reached for the tequila bottle and poured three more shots, which we all slammed down.

"So how did you come to have it?" I asked after I got my voice back from the tequila.

"I got it from my grandmother. I don't know how she got it, but she swore it was the real thing and..." Rita looked around again though it was still only the three of us in the bar able to hear her. "...she told me that because of this, Tiburcio's ghost can't rest. He wanders around looking for his lost parts."

"Okay! Now I know it's Bullshit!" I said, laughing. "Ghosts! You almost had me there until the ghosts. Good story though!"

Dave, still looking serious, said, "You know they used to bury the heads and bodies separately after the guillotine. They buried the bodies at crossroads so that the ghosts wouldn't know which way to go to look for their heads. People still swear they meet headless ghosts wandering around on moonless nights."

I looked from Dave to Rita and back, wondering if there was some kind of conspiracy between them to put me on, but if there was it sure didn't show. Their grave expressions suddenly sent a chill up my back, but I put on a brave front. "Okay, so where is this ghost wandering around? Where's he buried? San Jose, right?"

Rita nodded. "But his ghost isn't there; it's here in Agua Dulce where he was betrayed. At Vasquez's Rocks."

I blinked at her and the silence in the bar was like 90 weight motor oil poured over the three of us. Vasquez's Rocks is an immense, surreally up-thrusting castle of stone in the edge of the Mojave Desert. If you have ever seen an old cowboy movie or a science fiction TV show you've seen the place because this alien-seeming natural fortress has been used as outlaw hideout and extra-terrestrial locale since movies first came to Hollywood.

Dave nodded. "I've heard movie people say that place is haunted. Some of the crews and extras won't work out there after dark."

I looked back and forth between them, still thinking I was being had, but they both looked serious as a parson at a sinner's funeral. Still, I just couldn't buy into it. "Naw, this is Bull Shit! There's no ghost! And that's just a pickled mushroom or something, and this has been a great story and an interesting evening, but I'm gonna go home to Michele and sleep off this tequila." I started digging in my jeans pocket for my money clip to pay for my drinks when Rita said, "I betcha if you took this out there the ghost would come to you, then you'd believe me wouldn't you?"

"Yeah," Dave said, eyeballing me defiantly. "Then you'd believe her wouldn't cha?"

This time *I* reached over and poured us all another tequila, which we slammed down. Then I picked up the jar again and headed for the door. "You two coming?"

~ * ~

Vasquez's Rocks is a Los Angeles county park which closes at sunset unless you get permits which is what a lot of production companies do in order to shoot there at night, but the place isn't Fort Knox. Closed means a turnpike bar, that wouldn't keep out a kindergartner, is let down across the road. I parked with the nose of the car against the bar. We ducked under it and walked carefully into the open area in front of the 'castle' part of the formation. I was carrying the jar, which sat beside me on the car seat all the way down Highway 14, and I was feeling both a little silly and a little put upon. Besides which, I had a headache. Tequila and beer is not a good mixture for me.

We stood for a couple of minutes, and I finally called out, "Okay Vasquez, where-in-the-hell are ya? You want yer pud back, come and get it!"

Dave started shushing me. "What are you trying to do, get us arrested?"

"I'm just trying to prove to you there ain't no ghost." That's when I noticed Rita wasn't with us anymore. "Where'd she go? She's the one got us out here. What'd she do, run away?"

Out of the dark, Rita called, "Oye! Come here you two."

I couldn't exactly see her, but we followed the sound of her voice toward another part of the formation I knew pretty well. I used to bring my wife Michele up there before she was my wife. It was a nice private little place like an amphitheater scooped out of the solid stone with a wide bench at the back. It was away from the main part of the park, and on nights when the moon was bright, it was a pretty romantic spot. We'd park outside the gate, climb over and…well, you can guess from there.

When we got around the rock and inside the niche, it was so dark I couldn't see anything. "Where are you Rita?"

"I'm here. Come and sit down."

Annoyed but still willing to play along with the joke, I felt my way back to the bench with Dave right behind me. We sat and suddenly it was as though the dark little cavity in the rock had turned into a deep freeze. A silvery dot of light grew from a pinpoint to door size as though it was an aperture opening in the fabric of the night to let in an eerie crepuscular light.

I don't know what big Dave was doing, but I started shaking with more than cold and it was 'feets don't fail me now!' time, only my 'feets' did fail me. I couldn't move! I felt frozen to the bench with the supernatural cold. My eyes were bugging out as the spectral light coagulated into the figure of a man, tall and lanky, with a mop of jet-black hair and a huge drooping moustache. He probably would have been handsome except his head seemed crooked on his neck and his face was twisted with pain. He was dressed like a Mexican vaquero and was holding his wide round sombrero in front of him as though to shield his loins.

Fear was squeezing my chest so that I could hardly breath, but I managed to ask, "Who…who…are you?"

From somewhere, "Rio Rita" Vasquez stepped into the glow, was part of the glow! She lifted her hand and touched the tortured face of the ghost. "Te quiero Tiburcio," she said. Her voice was like the edge of a chisel drawn up my spine.

The ghost opened his arms to embrace her, and in doing so he moved the wide sombrero from his loins. The sight made me cringe with empathy, and I heard Dave gasp with the same emotion. The crotch of Tiburcio's brown pants was blood stained from his belt line to his knees.

Rita looked at us and her eyes turned my insides to water. "Bring it," she commanded, and her words lifted me from the bench to my feet. I stretched out my hand holding the jar, and Tiburcio took it from me. His touch was icy and malignant, and numbed my arm from fingertip to shoulder. I was being pulled into the glowing aperture and I was struggling to pull back when I felt big Dave's hands on the collar of my shirt and the seat of my pants, hauling me back from the supernatural trap. He dragged me out of the niche, and just outside it, we took off at a dead run for the car. We jumped in and did not stop until we were in Lancaster.

A few days later, Dave and I went back out to where *The Hole in the Wall* had been and found the place had burned down. There was nothing left but some charred sticks, and truth be told, they looked like they had been there for a hundred years.

What really happened that night I do not know, though Dave and I have talked it over a lot. Did we really see the ghost of Tiburcio Vasquez? And what the hell was Rita? Was she a ghost too? Maybe the ghost of Rosaria Leiva? But if it was Rosaria why didn't she just take the jar down to Vasquez's Rocks herself?

"Maybe she wasn't able," Dave said. "You got it down to look closer at it and you carried it when we went up there. She never touched it."

Maybe he's right. Maybe she couldn't, or maybe it was some kind of ghost conspiracy to catch a couple of live ones and she was the bait. At any rate that's the story and it still scares the bejesus out of me when I think about it, but every time Dave and I have talked about it since, we always end up saying "Too bad *The Hole in the Wall* is gone though. It was a great bar."

THE END

THE WINDS OF THE GREAT MOJAVE

The wind doesn't always blow in Southern California's Antelope Valley, but it blows often enough that most of the trees lean, having been blown sideways since they were sprouts. Very often the wind rolls in from the nearby Mojave Desert and when the hot, dry Mojave wind blows it stirs speculation in romantic hearts as to where that wind comes from. Of course there are all the scientific answers—uneven heating of the ground; rotation of the planet; seasonal considerations—but romantic hearts know that those are only facts not reasons.

There are speculations that the winds are caused by the Native American wind spirits who live in caves back in the mountains and blow when they are angry about something. That might be, especially the Santa Ana winds which blow down the canyons of the San Gabriel Mountains and scorch the Los Angeles basin making the yearly brush fires rolling hell. Those ancient spirits are probably angry with the white men who have supplanted the native peoples that left their hand prints and other marks on some of the standing stones in the great Mojave.

There are those who have left the Los Angeles basin to live in what used to be the more rural surroundings of the Antelope Valley and the great Mojave. If you ask them you will often hear the winds are caused by Los Angeles sucking, and they may not be wrong, but I believe I have located the source of at least some of the winds.

Back a while ago when gasoline was cheaper than bourbon, I found myself in little bar in the desert city of Mojave. Now Mojave wasn't much at the time. Still isn't for that matter. It is mostly a strip of gas stations, motels and eateries along the north bound highways, but it is also the home of desert rats and dreamers who look for gold in the rocks and in outer space. It is the home of the first privately owned space port in the country. The bar was called The Windy City Saloon. It was owned and run by a fellow named Jimmy Mills who was from Chicago, hence the name of the joint and the irony of the name did not escape him. Nor was it lost on me as I stepped out of the wind into the dim confines of the bar. It was mid-morning, so Jimmy and I were the only ones in the place as I seated myself at the bar and ordered a beer.

"Windy, ain't it?" I said, just to get the conversation going.

Jimmy was polishing glasses and didn't even look up when he said, "'bout like usual."

I blinked at him. "Usual?" I asked. "The wind's near strong enough to lift a skinny guy right off his feet. It was rolling a fifty-five gallon steel drum down the middle of the street."

"Empty?" he asked.

Again I blinked at him. "Yeah, I'm pretty sure," I said with just the slightest sarcastic twist in my voice.

"Nothing to that. One time I was putting gasoline in my pickup truck up at the Oasis general store and I saw this fifty-five gallon barrel rolling and bouncing along in the wind. It was striking sparks off the pavement and it got just a little bit passed the Oasis when it finally cracked open. One of the sparks popped and that barrel exploded. Threw fire all over the street. It'd been full of kerosene. If it had blown back another fifty yards, me and the Oasis would have been bar-b-qued."

Now a fifty-five gallon steel drum of kerosene would have to weigh in the neighborhood of five hundred pounds, but I didn't figure it was polite to call the man a liar right in his own bar so I just said, "Ah, Yeah." And sipped at my beer a little.

About that time another fellow blew in the door in a cloud of dust. He was an older fellow that would have fit into the desert rat category. He was dressed in stained jeans, cowboy shirt and a wind defying Stetson that looked older than me. Jimmy greeted him with, "Hey, Clyde," and started drawing a beer without being told. Clyde sat down at the bar with one stool between us and tipped his hat back. Jimmy set the beer glass in front of him and waited while he took his first sip before he said, "I just told this fella here about that drum of Kerosene that blew away and exploded, and I don't think he believes me."

Clyde glanced at me out of the corner of his eye then shook his head. "I ain't surprised. Hard to believe if you ain't seen how the wind can blow out here. Why just the other day I was driving down towards Rosamond when a half a hod of bricks blew across the road right in front of me."

I laughed. "Why Mister Clyde, you wouldn't fib to a poor pilgrim would you?"

He turned full face to me looking serious and offended. "Couple even hit the side of the truck. Made big ol' dents. I'm just lucky one of 'em didn't hit the windshield. It would have probably killed me. You want to come out and have a look?"

"No, no." I shook my head and raised my hands palm out. "Sorry if I offended. Didn't mean to doubt you."

"Hump" he snorted and went back to sipping his beer.

"You know," I began, trying to smooth over my faux paux, "I have heard the reason there are no antelopes in the Antelope Valley is because the wind blew 'em all over into Berdoo County."

Jimmy snorted and asked if I wanted another beer. As he was drawing it another cowboy/desert rat looking guy came in and brought the smell of sweated leather and horse manure with him. He was a long rawboned individual that looked like he spent lots of time out in the sun. Once again Jimmy drew a beer and set it down in front of the man without being told, then said, "Charles, this fella thinks this little breeze is a real wind. Can you imagine that?"

Charles looked me over with barely restrained contempt. "Why this ain't even an anvil wind," he said.

I should have kept my mouth shut and I knew it, but maybe it was my second beer that caused me to say, "Anvil wind?"

"Yep."

I should have left it alone but my mouth was suddenly leading a life all its own and I asked, "What's an anvil wind?"

He sipped his beer and said, "Well ya see, most times a horse that has been what ya call drop trained, that means they been trained to stand when you drop their reins on the ground, most times they'll just stand like they been trained. Out here the wind picks up the reins and makes that horse think it's being led and it can wander off to Lord knows where. A lot of places puts out weights to tie the reins too. Little breeze like is blowing now them weights is enough, but if the wind gets up, them little weights just blow on out straight at the end of the reins and the horse wanders, so some folks put out anvils to tie the horse reins too, but I seen the wind so high one time..."

"It picked up the anvil and led the horse off," I contemptuously finished the story for him.

He looked at me and, with disgust in his voice and a perfectly straight face said, "Didn't pick up the anvil, but it was scooting it along the ground. I followed the track it left to find the horse."

I shook my head and took another sip of beer, trying to wash the story out of my mind.

While Charles was telling his story, another man had come in. He was about my age and dressed in striped overalls. He had a sweat-stained red bandana tied around his neck and was wearing what I have always thought of as a train engineer's cap. "Cheese burger and a beer, Jimmy," he said.

Jimmy spoke through a little window behind the bar to the cook in back and drew the tap beer. The man sipped at the beer and listened to Charles finish his story and nodded. "Yep, I seen it that windy a lot of times," he volunteered. "But the worst I ever saw was when the wind caused Edwards Air Force Base to scramble fighter jets because they thought flying saucers were landing."

Once more I just could not help myself. I asked, "How's that?"

"Well see, I work just the other side of the tracks, over where they make train wheels. Now them wheels are might nigh as tall as I am and heavy as hell. Near a ton each. When we finish the wheels, before we put them on the axles and ship 'em we just put the wheels out in the big yard by the tracks. So one time we had a big contract with maybe a hundred wheels lying out there, when this big wind came up. It tore up houses and all kinds things and worst of all it picked up a bunch of them train wheels and flung 'em like Frisbees right over the mountain and across the dry lake beds at Edwards. They showed up on the radar over there and, since the Space Shuttle lands over there and Edwards does so much testing of new airplanes, some of 'em real secret, they thought they were being attacked by flying saucers. They scrambled fighter jets and shot down three train wheels before they discovered what they were."

I glanced at Jimmy and then at the other three unsmiling men in the bar. I'd had enough. I stood up, dug a ten dollar bill out of my pocket and threw it on the bar. "Keep the change, Jimmy," I said, and made my way out into the breeze.

Many people think the winds of the great Mojave come from the uneven heating of the planet, or the suction of Los Angeles' sprawl, but I think they come from the ancient wind spirits, and those spirits dwell in a little bar called The Windy City Saloon.

THE END

SLEEPING BEAUTY

Back a while ago, I was sitting with my friend Big Dave Dodge in a bar called Mickey's Mousehole sipping beer and half listening to the Dodgers lose on the TV. Now Big Dave is a man who is always interesting. He is called Big Dave because he is…well, big, and coming from me that means something since I am six three and weigh two forty. Dave stands six-six and weighs two seventy, and all of it looks mean. He rides a chopped Harley and looks like a Hells Angel with long hair and beard and, truth be told, he used to run with some pretty bad folks when he was younger, but now he keeps his 'Crazy Ass Biker' look because it generally makes for a peaceful existence and gets him bit parts on TV and in the movies.

When the inning ended an ad for Disneyland Vacations came on and suddenly Mickey the bartender spun away from where he was wiping glasses, threw his towel at the TV screen and screamed, "Fuck Mickey Mouse! And may Walt Disney Rot in hell!"

Regular customers of the Mousehole understood what that was all about. Michael Haggerty III hated Mickey Mouse and Walt Disney with a passion because Disney Corporation and its famous trade mark

17

infringement law department sued Haggerty for calling his bar Mickey's Mousehole. The Disney Corporation, which seldom loses, lost that one though, because the Mousehole had been called 'the Mousehole' since Prohibition when Michael Haggerty Sr. ran it as a Speak Easy before there was a Mickey Mouse. Now Michael Haggerty III, who had been called Mickey since he was in diapers, ran the joint and therefore had a certain claim to the name. But win or not the law suit cost Mickey a lot of money and great deal of hassle, so he hated Walt Disney and Mickey Mouse.

Big Dave looked thoughtful after Mickey's outburst. He was a man of poetical and philosophical disposition so I wasn't much surprised when he said, "I've heard that they froze his corpse."

"Who, Disney?"

"Yeah."

"I heard that too. Wonder if it's true."

Dave shrugged. "Probably. I mean they froze Ted Williams."

"Just his head."

"Yeah, just his head. I bet if they froze ol' Uncle Walt they froze his whole body."

"I reckon."

We sat and sipped beer for a bit, letting the idea of a Walt Disney Popsicle roll around in our minds until a question popped into my head. "Dave, where did they put 'im after they froze him?"

Dave took a big pull at his beer then said, "Well, I've heard rumors around a few movie sets that he's in a cryonic tank in a room like a safe under Disneyland."

"Really?"

Dave shrugged. "That's what I've heard. I even heard that was one of the reasons for the management shakeup in Disney. Michael Eisner supposedly wanted access to the cryonic room and Uncle Walt's family wouldn't let him have it."

"Really?" I asked again. I can be a real brilliant conversationalist sometimes.

"Naw, it's probably crap, but I have heard some stories."

"Like what?"

"Like that Eisner hired lawyers and tried to take control of the vault and when that didn't work he hired some private detectives to break into the place, and Roy Disney, Walt's nephew, hired a private army to keep Eisner out. Supposedly they are still there guarding the place."

"You mean some of those guys dressed up in the cartoon suits down there are really armed guards assigned to protect the cryonic tank where Walt's stored?"

Dave laughed. "I can just see Goofy running around with an assault rifle mowing down kids standing in line at Small World."

We both laughed at that and when we told Mickey what we were laughing about, he laughed too and once more said "Fuck Mickey Mouse!" before going back to wiping glasses.

Big Dave and I sipped beer a little more and watched the Dodgers finish getting their butts kicked before I said, "So where is this cryonic tank supposed to be?"

"Don't know, but I can guess."

"Under the Haunted Mansion? Is one of those floating heads really Uncle Walt in disguise?"

"Naw that would imply that he's dead and if he's frozen he ain't dead…"

"Course he's dead. They can't freeze a guy that isn't dead, it'd be murder."

"Yeah, yeah, in the real world, but we're talking about the World of Crazy Disney Worshipers."

"Okay, okay, so he isn't dead. Then where is he?"

"Under Sleeping Beauty's Castle of course."

I let that sink in for a little bit and said, "Yeah, That does kinda make sense. He was supposed to have an apartment in that castle in case he wanted to stay over, so it does seem right. Uncle Walt all stretched out under the castle waiting for some prince of a doctor to come and give him a medicated kiss to wake him up."

Dave laughed. "You got a very bizarre mind, brother Helm. Very bizarre indeed."

"Yeah, and look who's talking," I answered back and we both laughed.

~ * ~

A couple of months later when I got roped into taking my grandkids to 'The happiest place on earth,' I found my thoughts drifting back to that conversation in the Mousehole. I had sent Granny Michele and the kids off to stand in line for Space Mountain and I was sitting on a bench on Main Street looking up at the sun sparkling off the pointy tower of Sleeping Beauty's Castle, and I said to myself, *I wonder?*

Understand that I don't usually go out of my way to get into trouble, but I was hot and bored and tired of being elbowed by the hoi polloi so I decided I was gonna go find out if there really were armed Goofies hovering around Uncle Walt's tomb.

Now if Big Dave had been there, he probably would have tried to talk me out of the whole adventure because he is a lot more level headed than he looks. He has spent a lot of time hauling my skinny rear out of trouble for which I had no one to blame but myself, but he wasn't there, so I slugged down the rest of my lime soda wishing it was fortified with tequila and started for the castle.

I got as far as halfway across the bridge and stopped to figure my next move. There are a lot of mock-arrow slits and windows up higher on the castle walls, but down on the ground there are passages that go around under the eaves of the place and under those eaves there are stores trying to separate the visitors to the Magic Kingdom from their last dollar. *No apparent secret passages of any kind*, I thought. *but then if they were apparent they wouldn't be secret would they?* So I walked around the arcades looking in all the windows and watching the people flow by.

After I walked around the castle for fifteen or twenty minutes, I happened to notice one of the costumed characters coming along. It was Mickey Mouse himself and he was being carried along by the flowing crowd, apparently going about his job of amusing the kids while the vendors picked their pockets, but suddenly Mickey cut across the crowd and stopped beside a stand selling hats. It was one of those places that look like a kind of fairy tale building, made of logs and stone, and between the hat shop and the drinks stand beside it, there was a space of what appeared to be blank wall. Mickey stood with his back to the wall for a bit then he looked left and right, and when he was sure no one was watching, he leaned hard against the wall and it swung inward like a door. Mickey slid through, and the door quickly closed behind him.

Wellie, well well, I thought. *There is a secret passage.* Don't ask me why it didn't occur to me it might have been a secret door to a dressing room or a bathroom for costumed characters, but the idea never crossed my mind. When I saw Mickey disappear through that secret door, I knew it was the door to Walt's crypt.

I worked my way over to the blank wall between the hat shop and the drinks stand and leaned against it like Mickey did. Nothing happened. It was like I was leaning against a plaster wall. Maybe there was a secret word or something but if there was, I hadn't heard Mickey utter it, so I stepped back into the crowd and studied the wall as best I could. It was painted like mason-carved stone set into a wall, and no straight edge of a door showed, nor was there a knob, knocker, or bell of any kind, but when I brought my gaze to the ground in front of the wall, there was a small round brass thing that might have been a sewer cleanout or access to the fire sprinklers, but didn't look like either of those.

With a mental shrug, I positioned myself against the wall like Mickey had, making sure my heel was on that brass plate. I leaned my weight on it and put my back flatter against the wall. Nothing happened so I picked up my heel and started to step away, when a kid who should have been watching where he was going but wasn't, bashed into me, and I stepped back onto the brass plate. I felt, more than heard, a solid click beneath my foot and suddenly I was inside the door and it was closed behind me.

It wasn't the crypt. It wasn't even a long dark passage to the crypt. It looked more like a military or cop break room, with several large tables scattered around, and several men with crew cuts and blue and white uniforms sitting around them. They all wore side arms, but they were obviously taking a break to drink coffee and maybe eat a doughnut. They looked more surprised to see me than I was to see them. At a table on my left, Mickey Mouse, sans his mouse head, was standing with one foot up on a bench. The Mickey head sat on the table in front of him.

After a moment of stunned silence, one of the uniformed men with silver Lieutenant bars on his epaulettes stood up and came over to me. He looked like something out of a Sgt. Rock Comic book complete with crew cut and steely blue eyes in a craggy face. "Can I help you?" he asked, then went on, "You aren't supposed to be in here."

I opened and closed my mouth a couple of times before I managed to say, "I was just leaning on the wall waiting to buy some mouse ears for my grandkids, and some kid plowed into me, and here I am. Where am I?"

"Security coffee room," the lieutenant said.

"Oh. Okay. How do I get back out? I still need mouse ears."

~ * ~

A couple of days later I was back in the Mousehole telling Big Dave about my adventures. He was laughing so hard he almost fell off his stool, and even Mickey was laughing so hard he forgot to curse that wretched cartoon mouse.

"You didn't really figure you were gonna just walk into the crypt right off the thoroughfare, did ya? I mean everybody knows Disneyland has its own cops and they gotta take a break somewhere. Besides, there's miles of tunnels and underground rooms under Disneyland. Where do you think they stash all the machinery that makes Small World go round and round and stuff, and they sure ain't gonna put Uncle Walt anywhere he can be got to by some fool buying mouse ears. What were you thinkin' about?"

"I don't know what I was thinking, Dave. I was hot and bored, and the thought of armed Goofies standing guard around Walt's fridge was just too much. I couldn't help it."

That set off another gale of laughter with Mickey saying "Armed Goofies!" between guffaws.

I suddenly stopped laughing. Something I had seen but not noted had driven through the fog to my conscious mind. "All those guys were wearing BlackHorse patches on their sleeves," I said.

Dave stopped laughing too, then blinked and said, "BlackHorse? You sure?"

I thought about it a little more and then said, "Yeah. BlackHorse. They were all wearing BlackHorse Patches."

"Now why would Disney security guards be wearing BlackHorse patches?" Mickey asked

"Yeah, And why would Disney hire one of the largest para-military organizations in the world as security for Disneyland?"

BlackHorse was a "security company" like Standard Oil was a "Gas Station." It was a worldwide company that, depending who you talked too, was "private security" or a mercenary army. The American Government had hired BlackHorse to secure the gates of American military bases all over the United States, and the CIA had purportedly hired them to stir up a minor coup in Central America. The company had been put together by a couple of retired Air Cav Generals, hence the name BlackHorse.

"You don't suppose there is more down under Disneyland than a Walt Disney Popsicle do you?" I asked.

Dave shrugged. "Maybe. But BlackHorse is famous for its willingness to do anything for money, so maybe Disney just paid them enough to guard Walt's freezer."

We all three stared into our glasses and considered for a while. At last Mickey said, "Boys you can do what you want about finding out what's under Disneyland, but leave me out of it. I've had all the Disney I can stand."

"Maybe we should all forget about it," Dave said.

Now I am a man of questioning nature. I like to know what makes things work and I especially like trying to unravel conspiracies, and this whole Disney thing had tickled my conspiracy bone from the beginning. Now that conspiracy bone was fairly jumping out my chest with curiosity. "There has got to be a way to get down under that castle without the armed Goofies noticing."

Big Dave, also a man intrigued by conspiracies, scratched his chin thoughtfully and said, "I need to ask some questions from some folks I used to know."

So that is how I wound up crouched behind a huge air conditioning vent pipe, looking at a firmly locked steel door guarded by two

BlackHorse soldiers dressed in urban camouflage when all hell broke loose.

Dave talked to some actor friends who were putting together a show for the Main Street Theater inside Disneyland, and they listed us as stage grunts, so we just waltzed in without as much as a blink from the gate security guys. The rehearsal started late because of the crowd of Disneyland visitors and that worked fine for us. We came in under cover of darkness and split off from the actors unnoticed.

We did a recon on the park as the crowd thinned, looking for go-downs to get into the depths below and were about to give it up when we saw a BlackHorse uniformed man stop beside one of the huge red trash receptacles in Fantasyland over by the Merry-go-round. He looked all around, but it was late, so there were not many people left in the park. We were standing in the shadows so he didn't see us. He put his hand inside the mouth of the trash receptacle and the side of it swung open. There was a light coming from inside so that we could see a winding steel staircase, then the guard stepped through and pulled the door/trash receptacle closed behind him.

"Might be another break room or something," I said, remembering all too well the last time I stepped through a hidden door.

"Might be, but we gotta get in and go down somehow and this and your break room are the only ways I know."

"Yeah. Okay, let's go."

We looked all around then stepped to the receptacle. I put my hand in the opening just as the guard had and found a button. "What if it rings a bell down below or something?" I asked.

Dave shrugged. "Push it. Been a long time since I played 'ring and run.' "

So I did.

The door popped open and let a splash of ashy looking florescent light slant out, followed by the damp musty smell of enclosed concrete rooms.

If the button rang a bell below or some such we didn't hear it, and when we stepped inside onto the stair landing, we waited a couple of moments to see if someone was going to challenge us. Nobody did so we began to ease down the spiraling staircase. Looking over the side we could see that the stairs went a long way down. It looked like several stories, and every twelve steps there were openings out into the underground levels.

"How do we know where to get off, Dave?" I whispered.

"Gotta be at the bottom. If I was Uncle Walt I would put my crypt at the very bottom…"

"…But still under the castle."

Dave nodded.

"How we gonna find the castle? I'm all turned around."

"That way." He pointed. "When we get to the bottom, we go that way." Which we did.

The vaults underneath the Magic Kingdom are amazing. There are power vaults and gas mains and hydraulic pumps and lines and sewage pumps and lines, air conditioning ducts. Pipes and conduits of every size imaginable, from no larger than your pinky finger to big enough that Dave could have stood inside without having to bend over, and all that piping made for a really confusing trek, but Dave seemed to know where he was headed, and I just kept tagging along.

The sound of voices echoing down the corridor slowed us to a creep. We could see that the corridor broadened into a wider room at the end, but we couldn't see anyone in there. When we got to the end of the corridor, I laid down on the ground and slowly put my head around the corner. Two air conditioning ducts dipped and curved in front of me but left an inch or so of space between them and the floor, so I could see under them to the afore mentioned steel door. The guards were standing at ease and talking quietly. I could hear their voices but couldn't understand what they were saying.

I scooted around the corner still hidden by the curve of the AC ducts and signaled for Dave to follow. He'd barely gotten around the corner and out of sight when a flash followed by a loud BANG went off. It was so bright and so loud I saw stars, and my ear drums felt like they had burst. I can't imagine what it would have been like if we had not been protected from some of the effect by the AC ducts. We would probably have been left screaming and dazed like the guards at the door. As it was I was stunned almost immobile, but I tried to scramble over Dave and back the way we had come. He grabbed me by the shirt collar and shoved me back, then motioned for me to sit still and be quiet. A second later I was glad he had, because about twenty men all dressed in black and armed with assault rifles came pounding out of that corridor. They were so focused on their target that they didn't notice us, but I would have run head long into them if Dave hadn't grabbed me.

We both lay down and looked through the space under the AC duct at the steel door. Probably fifty armed soldiers now milled around in front. They were establishing a perimeter facing outward from the steel door. Now that I could see it better, I noticed a key pad of some kind on the left side, but the men who were standing beside the door weren't worrying about that. They were placing some kind of plastic explosive on the door and after a moment, one man with a twist igniter gave it a spin and the plastic charge went BOOM. In a moment the smoke cleared, and two of the men laid shoulders to the door. It didn't give at first but the second bash moved it a little and the third bash popped it all the way open.

Between the smoke and the noise and the guns I was about to pee my pants. I'd been around more guns and explosions than I care to remember when I was in the Army, but that didn't make me less scared of them. All I could do was lay there and watch as a squad of four guys went through the breached door, and came out in a couple of seconds pushing a thing that looked like a big black coffin on a four wheeled cart. Steam fumed off the box like fog rolling off dry ice, and the guys pushing all wore huge gloves.

"What the fuck?" Dave said, but if he had anything more to say it got lost in the sound of assault rifle fire that poured in from the left front of us, and I went from 'about to pee' to 'has peed.'

The assault team that breached the door, except the four guys pushing the coffin, turned and answered fire. The four guys pushing the coffin ran toward the corridor Dave and I had come down, and when they were sheltered behind pipes and concrete walls and headed on down the corridor, the rest of the assault team began to retreat. They were still throwing shots back up the hall, and those were being answered. I could hear slugs bouncing and ricocheting around us and the bitterness of ignited cordite made my eyes tear and my nose run.

The assault team pulled back two or three at a time and followed the coffin down the corridor. At last the final two guys pulled back and knelt beside us, using the AC ducts for cover. One of them noticed us for the first time and swung his rifle toward us. If I hadn't already wet my pants, I would have then for sure, but I had, so all Dave and I could do was stick our hands up and hope this guy didn't shoot.

He took one look at us and must have decided we were no threat, because he turned back toward the other firing, let go a couple of short bursts and then he and his partner hauled ass down the corridor.

I got to my knees and tried to follow him, but once more Dave grabbed me and pulled me to the floor. Good thing too, because in another second, a half dozen heavily armed BlackHorse guards came pounding across in front of the blown door. They stopped beside our hiding place and threw more shots down the corridor after the guys in black, then a couple of them moved cautiously on down the corridor, leaving the others behind. One of them, a guy with Sergeant's stripes below his BlackHorse patch, was talking into a hand held radio, but my ears were roaring so loud I couldn't make out what he was saying.

One of the BlackHorse guys who had been firing down the corridor lowered his rifle and looked around, and there we were. Dave and I laying in a puddle of my urine with our hands up praying this guy wouldn't shoot us either. He didn't. Instead he tapped the sergeant on the arm and pointed at us. The Sergeant looked down at us, did a double take and said, "Dave? What the hell are you doing here?"

~ * ~

There is a joke about a guy named Willy who is known by everyone in the world. Now Dave isn't Willy, but he is known by a remarkable number of people, and boy was I glad this sergeant was one of them. I don't know that they would have shot us and disposed of the bodies in some underground sump there beneath Disneyland, but I got the feeling that if Matt Clemens hadn't known Dave, it might have been a distinct possibility. As it was Sgt. Clemens had his men frog march us to a little room that looked very much like an interrogation cell. It had a table and two chairs, and when I looked around, I found a camera up in one corner so our captors could keep an eye on us. We weren't manacled or shackled, but the table was fixed in place and there were eye bolts underneath to hook hand cuffs to if we had been.

Dave and I sat silently for a while just looking at the gray concrete walls and thinking our own thoughts, but at last I said, "Thank God that guy knew you. And how *does* he know you anyway?"

"From the movies. He's worked as an extra with me several times. I knew he worked in security, but I didn't know he was BlackHorse."

I shook my head in disbelief. "Is everybody in Southern California connected with the movies?"

Dave shrugged.

"How much trouble you think we're in here, Dave?"

Again with the shrug. "They might get us for trespassing, or maybe even breaking and entering, if they decide to have some law into this, but they aren't exactly in the clear themselves. Armed private militia is sorta frowned on by local and federal authorities, if ya know what I mean."

I thought about that for a little while and looked at the windowless walls and the locked door.

"What the hell happened out there?"

Dave shook his head. "I don't know, but I got the feeling it wasn't an intra-corporate disagreement."

About then Sgt. Clemens and the Lieutenant from the coffee room incident came in. The Lieutenant, whose name was Nickelson, glared at us looking like a housewife finding weevils in her flour, and he seemed to pay special attention to me, but at last he said, "Okay you two, what the hell are you doing down here?"

Dave and I both started to talk at once. The Lieutenant stopped us short and pointed at me. "You tell me, Mouse Ears," he growled.

I'm sure I blushed at being recognized because I suddenly got hot all over and my mouth got even drier than it already was, but I managed to stammer out, "Well, one day Dave and me were sitting in Mickey's bar..."

Clemens and the Lieutenant listened with remarkable patience to my story and shook their heads in utter disbelief when I came to the end.

"So you don't know anything about the guys that took the...the assault team?" the Lieutenant asked.

"No sir," I answered. His lieutenant's bars and steel blue eyes brought all the old military habits right up to the top.

"How 'bout you?" He asked Dave.

"No idea."

I said, "I swear to God we won't tell anybody anything about anything, if you'll just let us out of here, Sir," but Dave was braver, or maybe more curious. He asked, "Do you guys have any idea who they were?"

They both looked us over for a long second, still considering whether to simply shoot us I'm sure, but finally the Lieutenant said, "Clemens, do you really know this guy?"

"Yes sir."

"And you'll vouch for him?"

Clemens ran eyes up and down Dave and then me. "Yes sir. I'll vouch for him…for the both of them. Nobody would believe them anyway, probably."

"It is pretty wild, you gotta admit," Dave said.

"Yeah. Pretty wild," I agreed, which drew a withering look from the lieutenant.

"So who shot up your crypt?" Dave prodded.

The Lieutenant took a deep breath then let it out and began:

"This whole thing, the cryonic crypt and all, has been an urban legend since Disney died and you guys aren't the first people who have tried to find out if it was true, but usually they get picked up before they ever get close to the security door. Even the couple who have made it as far as the door have only ever seen the guards and the door before we picked them up and handed them over to the Anaheim police. There are some more urban legends that go along with the crypt. I mean, Disney is supposed to have had a whole new world order mapped out and was financing it all through Disney Corporation, using his movies and the amusement parks to pervert the youth of the world. So after Walt died some of the family supposedly took over, and the organization still exists. They are allegedly funding cryonic research and underground revolutionary groups all over the world who are working to bring this Disney World Order into being, and when the world order is in place they are gonna bring Walt back from his freezer to be the emperor of the world or something. It's crap of course, but harmless crap, or at least I thought it was until about a year ago when BlackHorse got this contract. The Disney people showed us all these threatening letters and gave us the names of a bunch of pretty big people that apparently believe in this Disney World Order thing. They call it the 'DWO threat.' It is just mind boggling! There are web sites and organizations that send out literature talking about the 'DWO threat' and how it advocates the violent overthrow of the United States government. It's just nuts! Even the Disney people thought it was harmless foolishness until a couple of armed crazies stormed the guard gates one night..."

"Hey, I remember that!" I said. "They took a bunch of people hostage and held 'em for several hours. I thought it was some kind of robbery gone wrong."

"Yeah, that was the story Disney and the Police let out, and since the SWAT team killed both the perps, there was no-one left to say different," Clemens said.

"And that was when Disney called BlackHorse," the Lieutenant finished.

"Wow," Dave said. "I knew the Disney Corporation had enemies. I mean they've pissed a lot of people off with copyright lawsuits and stuff, but I didn't know it had gone this far."

Through all this explanation there was still only one question running through my mind and it would *not* stay unasked. I tried to keep my mouth shut, but it was like trying to hold a mouthful of hot soup. Against my will it came bursting out:

"So that really was Disney in that box those other guys got?"

It was like I had set off a flash-bang in the room! All eyes including Big Dave's clapped onto me, and the sound of a pin being dropped would have been like an explosion.

The lieutenant came out of it first and said, "I can neither confirm nor deny the truth of that statement."

"But..." I started and Dave, good old smart, calm Dave, grabbed my arm and said. "Shut up, G."

"But..."

With slightly clenched jaws, Dave went on, "It was something valuable enough the Disney Corporation was willing to pay BlackHorse to guard it, so just let it go at that. Otherwise these gentlemen might have to reconsider our position here."

I had taken a breath to protest some more when Dave's meaning got through my thick skull and I said, "Oh, yeah," and shut my big flappy mouth."

The tension took a while to drain out of the room, but at last Dave asked, "So, you got any idea who this raiding party was?"

I suddenly had a funny feeling in my belly.

"Not a clue," the lieutenant said, "but you can bet your ass BlackHorse investigations is going to find out who done it. Disney is gonna want their...want that box back and BlackHorse is gonna get it for them."

~ * ~

Dawn was just pinking the eastern sky when Sgt. Clemens ushered us through the same back gate we'd come through a few hours before. "You guys came away lucky," he said. "I don't know for sure that Nickelson would have killed you, but I wouldn't put it past him. He has a reputation as a bad ass so I don't know. But if I was you I wouldn't ever set foot on Disney Property again."

"I think that's good advice" Dave said. He stuck his hand out toward Clemens. "Thanks Matt. If I can ever return the favor let me know." Clemens shook his hand and then mine, and I echoed what Dave had said.

Clemens said, "Dave, you know a lot of people all over the place. Kinda keep an ear open about this, okay? And for God sakes, keep your mouths shut."

"Sure Matt. If I hear anything, you'll be the first to know, and I have already forgotten the last few hours."

"Me too," I added.

Dave narrowed his eyes thoughtfully. "You think maybe these guys took the box to hold it for ransom?"

"I don't know," Clemens said, then added, "… and you don't wanna know. You got me?"

This time it was my turn to do the saving. I grabbed Dave's upper arm and started to drag him away. His arm was like an iron bar. "Say good bye to the nice sergeant, Dave," I said, and pulled him after me as I walked away.

~ * ~

I caught hell when I got home. Michele is used to my weirdness of mind and of hours, but even that wouldn't just automatically make her forgive my staying out all night. She would probably have divorced me if we hadn't been married all these years. When I told her I was with Dave, she eased back some. She likes Dave and trusts him, though he and I have been in trouble before.

Still, she is a curious lady and she really wanted an explanation, for which I couldn't blame her, but I couldn't very well tell her we'd been skulking around underneath Disneyland, and been involved in an armed assault on Walt Disney's cryonic tomb, so I just told her we'd been drinking beer and telling stories at Dave's house and decided it wouldn't be safe for me to try to drive home. I caught some more hell of the "Well ya coulda called! I was worried to death!" kind, but much better she was beating me up with that than my trying to tell her what had really happened. It ended with her saying, "Thank God Dave had sense enough to keep you from trying to drive!" and I just nodded my agreement that Big Dave was a very good friend.

~ * ~

By mutual understanding Dave and I didn't go back to the Mousehole for a while. We didn't actually talk about it, we just didn't go. Instead we went to 'The Golden Gopher' the owner of which was a displaced Minnesotan and, so far as I know, the University had never sued him for using their team name, which was fine with me. So a couple of days after what Dave and I began calling 'The Disneyland Raid' we met in the Golden Gopher to begin our after action report and debrief.

"I been looking on-line," Dave began as soon as we had beer in front of us.

"Yeah, me too. I never heard of this DWO stuff before, but it sure is all over the Internet."

"Yeah, and did you happen to run across the blog one Mickey Haggerty runs?"

I took a deep breath and a sip of suds before I nodded. "I always knew Haggerty was nuts about Disney, but I didn't know he was into this DWO thing. I mean Damn! You'd think he believes Disney is the Antichrist or something."

Dave nodded. "I guess everybody has a right to be a little nuts about something, but what really gave me the yips was all the other people that were agreeing with him and writing their own craziness into it. Did you read the one about Disney having been connected with the Columbia crash?"

"Made my stomach turn over," I agreed. "It was so nuts it was plausible."

We looked at each other through the dimness of the bar lights for a moment shaking our heads, then we just sat and sipped beer for a little while. I am no mind reader, but it wasn't too hard to figure that Dave was thinking the same thing I was thinking. Wondering how deep into this Mickey Haggerty really was, and whether he had been involved in the raid to steal Disney's coffin...

"*If* it was Disney's coffin," Dave said in answer to my thought.

"You saw the steam rolling off it same as me, and I defy you to tell me what else they would be keeping in a freeze box like that."

"Yeah, you're right."

"And if Mickey was involved, how come he was so anxious for us to keep him out of it? Seems to me he'd be cheering us on trying to prove that what he's been saying in his blog was true," I said, but I knew the answer almost before I formed the question. It was the same answer that had given me the sinking feeling when Sgt. Clemens and Lt. Nickelson questioned us. Mickey Haggerty was in this up to his eyeballs.

We looked at each other across the table. Neither of us wanted to ask the next question, but finally I said, "Should we tell Clemens?"

"Mickey's a friend."

"Yeah, but Dave...I mean, *Disney World Order?*"

He scratched at his beard and sipped his beer, then broke the wet ring on the table where his glass had been with his finger tip. "Maybe we're just jumping to conclusions," he said at last. "And what do we care anyhow? I don't even like Mickey Mouse."

It wasn't much of a hope, but it was the only one I saw so I grabbed on to it. "Yeah," I said. "Yeah. What do I care if it was Walt in that box?"

We stalled a few more minutes finishing our beers, but when they were gone we both got up and headed out the door. Once more we hadn't as much as mentioned what we were about to do, but we both knew we were going to the Mousehole.

~ * ~

I really don't know how Haggerty stayed in business 'cause I don't ever remember the Mousehole being really crowded, and once more it was almost empty. There were a couple of old timers leaning on the bar as far away from the door as it was possible to get, but that was all. Mickey looked up when we pushed through the padded door.

"I thought you guys left town," he said, laughing.

"We're considering it," Dave said as we sat down on our favorite stools.

Mickey drew two from the tap and set them in front of us. "What'sa matter, Mickey Mouse chasing you?" he asked with a grin, but when both Dave and I flinched at the joke, Haggerty twigged that something was up. "You guys go looking for Uncle Walt's Ice Box like you were planning?"

"We know about the Blog and the Disney World Order and all of it Mickey," I said.

Mickey lifted an eyebrow then shrugged. "Just a hobby. Anything to needle the Disney Corporation."

"We got caught in the cross-fire, Mickey," Dave said.

Now Mickey stood up straight and said, "What cross fire?"

"The BlackHorse guys caught us and held us for like six hours. We didn't tell them anything because we didn't know about the blog and the DWO and all that. They let us go because they thought we were harmless, but they asked me to keep an eye out."

"They are gonna come after ya Mickey. They want that coffin back and BlackHorse is gonna come after you to get it," I said.

He flicked his eyes back and forth over us before he said, "They can't come after me if they don't know it's me. You guys gonna tell?"

"Hell Mickey, we aren't gonna have to tell," Dave said. "Disney has enough money they can pay BlackHorse and twenty other investigation services to go one by one through the blogs and websites till they come to you. I wouldn't even put it past 'em to get the government involved too."

Haggerty flicked his eyes back and forth over us again. A kind of a strange light came into them. It might have been fear, but I couldn't be sure. "Okay. What if I give it back?"

Dave thought a moment. "If you give it back and Uncle Walt hasn't thawed out any, I'd bet they would be willing to forget it, but I don't know."

"Besides, what are you gonna do with a Disney Popsicle anyhow, Mickey?" I asked and tried to laugh.

The corners of Haggerty's mouth turned up in a grin that I wasn't sure was because of my joke. "Yeah, your right." He turned his eyes to Dave. "Will you contact 'em for me?"

"I'll call Clemens," he said.

~ * ~

I don't know what Big Dave said to Clemens or Nickelson or whoever he talked to, but it was arranged. Dave didn't ever actually give Mickey's name or any other real information. Mickey told us he had the coffin stored in a freezer warehouse out in the valley and the temperature never changed more than a degree or two in the time he had it. We didn't ask anything about who the raiding party were or how they had gotten into Disneyland that night, just arranged for someone to show up in the parking lot of the freezer warehouse to pick up the box. Naturally they wanted to check the box out to see it hadn't been opened or whatever, but they said they were willing to just take the box after it had been inspected.

Dave explained this all to Mickey who didn't say much except, "No Cops, right?"

"Just BlackHorse and whatever techs and equipment they need to check the box."

"I gotta be there?"

"Yeah. You do, just in case the box isn't in the condition you promised. They aren't a trusting bunch."

"And what's to stop 'em from just grabbing me up along with the box?"

Dave shrugged. "I suppose you could get your raider buddies out there to cover the whole thing, but I don't think they want any trouble. I mean, they have gone out of their way for a long time to keep this whole 'Disney in a freezer' thing quiet, so I don't think they are gonna do anything to draw attention to themselves now."

"They might just kill me," Haggerty said, but he didn't sound much afraid of any such thing happening.

"I doubt they'll want to take the chance. They'd have to kill more than just you."

"Yeah," I said. "And Michele would be upset if my worthless ass got killed, so I wrote out the whole story and sent a copy to a friend of mine in the newspaper business…"

"And I sent a copy to a friend in the Screen Actors Guild, so if anything happens to any of us the whole crazy story is going to come out," Dave added.

So it was all set up. Mickey and Dave and I were gonna meet whoever BlackHorse sent in the parking lot. I thought I was gonna have to fight Dave before he would let me go. He first said, "No way! Michele would kill me if I let you go into this."

"She doesn't have to know."

He protested a little more but finally gave up and made me promise to stay back away from the exchange. I told him I'd stay back in the shadows, but I thought I could probably get up close to see better when the time came.

~ * ~

I am tempted to say that it was a 'dark and stormy night' the Wednesday night of the exchange but it wasn't. It was a typical fall night in the San Fernando Valley. Gin clear with sparkling stars and a slight breeze to keep the smog at bay. The freezer warehouse was one of a couple dozen buildings in an industrial park and the park was more empty than not. There were probably a couple of the manufacturing places in the park that were running night shifts but none of them were close enough to have much effect on us.

The three of us put on heavy gloves and carefully pushed the steaming box out of the freezer into the shadow of the building facing the parking lot. The box was still on its four wheeled cart, and cold enough that I could feel the incipient frost bite on my hands even through the gloves. As we pushed it, I saw that it was a sort of self-contained freezer unit with dials set into the top right underneath what looked like a window, so inspectors could look into it, or maybe so Walt could look out. I couldn't see anything because the glass was covered with kaleidoscopic ice crystals and I was pretty happy about that. I didn't really want to see Uncle Walt in his Popsicle state, as my dreams are strange enough without any such thing as that being added to them.

We stood in the shadow waiting and not talking. The parking lot was a long one with one entrance off the city street and several more off the alley across which we waited. The meeting was supposed to happen at ten o'clock, so about five of, we all began glancing at our watches and as the seconds ticked by, Dave and I grew steadily less able to stand still. Haggerty, on the other hand, stood as though this was just any old night. As I think back it was kinda spooky how calm he seemed.

At ten o'clock on the dot, two sets of headlights turned into the far end of the parking lot. One belonged to what looked like an ambulance and one belonged to a 'deuce and half' painted haze gray with a tarp stretched over its bed. As it got closer, we saw it had the BlackHorse symbol painted on the door. The two vehicles drew up opposite us, swung around and stopped, then four men came out of the ambulance, and half a dozen armed urban-camouflaged BlackHorse soldiers piled out of the truck. They didn't lower their weapons into assault configuration, but they held them across their chests at the ready.

Mickey, Dave, and I pushed the coffin out of the shadow toward the little group of men and when we were about five paces from them, we stopped and took a couple of paces back. The Disney guys from the ambulance came forward and Lt. Nickelson came with them. They all hovered around the box for a moment then one of the Disney guys appeared to wipe the little window. He was not satisfied so he wiped it again.

Mickey stepped forward as though he was going to have a look at the window, but the guy who had been wiping it said, "This thing has been opened! That's the only way it could get ice crystals on the inside of the window. You opened it!"

Mickey lifted his right hand to about waist high and moved it so we all could see that he had something in his hand, then shouted "FUCK MICKEY MOUSE!" and pushed the button.

There was some general that once said "there is no problem on earth that cannot be solved by the judicious application of high explosives." Apparently Mickey Haggerty was a devotee of that philosophy because when he pushed that button, some perfectly shaped charges of plastic explosive went BOOM and Walt Disney's freezer box went straight up into the air about fifty feet and hung there a moment, before a second explosion disintegrated it and whatever was inside it into ten million very small pieces.

The launching explosion had been so perfectly shaped even Nickelson and the four Disney guys who were standing right beside it were barely moved by the concussion. Their ears were probably ringing, but there was no other harm to them. Dave and I, at about ten feet away, didn't feel a thing, and when the second explosion went, it blew the box into so many pieces that when they reached us, it was as though we were being hit in the face by windblown sand.

Dave and I looked at each other and then at the place where Haggerty had been standing. He was gone. He'd used the explosions to divert attention while he ran back into the shadows and on into the night.

It took a moment for the BlackHorse squad to react, but when they did, they all aimed their guns at Big Dave and me. Our mouths dropped open even further than they already were and we raised our hands.

I don't know if it was the explosions or if Mickey arranged it, but within a couple of minutes police sirens and blinky lights were making rags of the clear night, and all of us ended up in LAPD custody. I don't know what anyone else told the cops but I mostly just kept my flap shut and plead not guilty at the bail hearing. By and by Michele showed up with a bail ticket and got me out. She didn't say anything as I collected my personal effects, and everything was pretty quiet as we drove home, but when we got in the front door she shook her head and looked at me with those forest pool brown eyes and said, "What in hell's name have you gotten yourself into?"

~ * ~

A few days passed and I didn't hear from Dave or anyone else. All I could do was sit and stew, and by turns curse Mickey Haggerty, Walt Disney, BlackHorse, and my own stupidity, and fight off the urge to laugh like a maniac at the whole mess. I got in touch with a lawyer who did what lawyers do and pretty soon told me all charges had been dropped and I owed him five hundred dollars. I called Dave and found out that the same thing happened to him. Apparently the Disney people had managed to grease whatever wheels justice still has to make LAPD and the courts forget about the big noise that happened on that Wednesday evening. Next day when I told Michele I was going down to the Golden Gopher to meet Dave, she put the gimlet eye on me and said, "You can get somebody else to bail you out next time," and I answered, "Yes Ma'am," and got out of there before she decided to throw something at me.

Dave was waiting with beer drawn when I got there. "Have you heard anything from Mickey?" I asked, sitting down across the table from him.

He shook his head. "He's probably in Mexico or something. Has anyone else tried to contact you?"

"No."

"Anybody watching your house or anything?"

That question gave me pause. "Not that I know of, why?"

"Have you looked at any of the DWO websites or blogs?"

I suddenly felt a nervous prickle on my neck and looked around to see only a couple of people and Gus the barkeep in the place, before carefully admitting that I had.

"All of 'em have links to the pix," I said. "I can't believe Mickey managed to get all those pix of the Popsicle and even a tape of the explosion."

Dave shook his head, and I could see he was having a hard time not breaking up laughing. He lifted his beer glass a little off the table and said, "To Mickey Haggerty, and the Mousehole."

I lifted my glass and clinked the rim against his and added, "Fuck Mickey Mouse."

THE END

ILLEGAL ALIENS

Big Dave and I tended to change bars every so often. We'd get bored or something would happen and we'd get eighty-sixed, or the bar would suddenly disappear like The Hole in the Wall or Mickey's Mousehole, but mostly we would just go looking for adventure at different places, which was how we ended up at the Windy City Saloon out in Mojave.

I found the Windy City on a trip through the city of Mojave during a time I lived at Edwards Air Force Base with my wife Master Sergeant Michele Helm. That was about the same time I first met Big Dave Dodge at the Hole in the Wall Bar which was out in the desert from Edwards. That meeting turned out to lead to interesting things, like running across, and running away from the ghost of Tiburcio Vasquez the Mexican bandit, and later discovering where Walt Disney was really buried, or stored like a Popsicle really.

Now Big Dave fits the name. Six foot six, two hundred seventy lbs. Long hair, long beard, sometimes braided sometimes not, dressed mostly in leather, denim, and motorcycle boots. He made a good deal of his living with his looks, playing wild bikers in the movies and on TV, but he was in fact not a Hells Angel or a Mongol or affiliated with any such outfit. He was a very gentle giant that made a little of his living writing greeting card poetry. Don't get me wrong, he was no pussy cat, but it took a lot to get his dander up. However, when it was up he was pretty much a force of nature. I once saw him lift a motorcycle over his head and throw it, granted it was a smallish bike, but still.

Anyway, Dave and I fetched up in the Windy City Saloon because I had told him about my first encounter there. It had been all about the wind and how strong it could get in the Antelope Valley and where it came from. When I told Dave I had been assured by people in the Windy City bar the wind had once gotten so high as to pick up steel train wheels and fling them over the mountain into Edwards AFB air space, and set off a panic because the wheels showed up like flying saucers on the Edwards Radar, he said "OH, HO, HO, this is a joint I gotta see."

Now the Windy City Saloon doesn't look like much. More hovel than building, but it was pretty much an institution with a wide variety of people. I met desert rats and cowboys and prospectors and makers of train wheels, and some of the most truly colossal liars I'd ever run into anywhere, which meant the conversation in the joint was always lively and interesting, so long as one didn't take it too seriously, or rather knew when to take it seriously and when not.

One evening Dave and I were sitting in the bar sipping beer and watching the TV hung up over in the corner. The thing was turned onto the History Channel or some such. See the Windy City ain't your typical bar with sports or such on the TV. During the baseball season you might catch a Dodger game or something, but most other times the channel stayed on History or National Geographic or one of the other information channels. Anyhow, the History Channel or something was on and they were talking about UFO's and ancient visitations by extra-terrestrial beings and space flights and marks left on walls that were supposed to have been left there by people who had actually had some kind of truck with the aliens when they were here. When a commercial hit Jimmy, the owner and bartender of the place, said, "There's a lot of those wall markings around here ya know? Over by Barstow at Fort Irwin there's a whole mess of 'em."

"Yeah, and up in the Red Rock country too." Earl, a regular denizen of the bar chimed in.

"Big cave up out of Tehachapi got lots of 'em too," I added. "I been up there. Long walk in though. California State Park Rangers do guided tours up there in the spring and fall."

"So what did the wall writing have to say," Dave asked and sucked in a swig of beer.

Clyde, another regular chimed in with, "Pro'bly said, 'Heap big flying saucer come down, et up all the Antelope in the Valley.' " This was a standard joke about the lack of antelopes anywhere in the Antelope Valley.

"Ya'll go on and scoff," a fella in stripped overalls and an engineer cap said. "I ain't so sure them ancient alien guys are wrong." I had met him before, but somehow had never caught his name. He was the one that worked in the train wheel factory over on the other side of Mojave who had told us about the train wheels setting off the UFO scramble over at Edwards.

"Awh, you don't believe that shit any more 'n I do," Jimmy said.

The other fellow shrugged. "Air Force believes it," he said.

"Ah, that's Bull shit." Clyde snorted and took a drink of beer.

"I promise ya it ain't, Clyde," I said. "There really is a protocol for UFO sightings. My wife used to have to deal with 'em sometimes when we still lived on base. I 'member once she didn't get back from work for two days because the US of A Air Force was out chasing lights in the sky. I saw 'em too. Half a dozen really bright balls of light looked like they were flying in formation over the Base. They came and went a mess of times. Scrambled fighters to chase 'em and everything."

"Bah," Clyde said. "Sun Dogs or something."

"I don't know, you could be right. I don't think they ever figured out what that was all about. By and bye the balls went away and that was the end of it."

Big Dave had mostly just been sitting and sipping as he listened to the TV and then to the back and forth, but now he said, "Maybe the UFO's missed their target. Maybe they were supposed to be doing recon on Area 51."

All of a sudden the bar got quiet. Everybody from around Mojave had heard of Area 51. It was supposed to be a super-secret test base for new air planes over in western Nevada and all the UFOlogists thought there was extra-terrestrial stuff being hidden and tested over there.

There had been reports, supposedly by people who worked over there, about flying saucers that scientists and engineers were tearing apart to find out about propulsion systems and skin covering systems and other stuff. There was a rumor the Stealth Technology that made American fighters invisible to radar came from what had been discovered in these hidden flying saucers.

People around Mojave and the Antelope Valley in general took anything that had to do with aerospace testing dead serious. The AV and Mojave were home to test flights and reaches into space from the old X 15 and Chuck Yeager to Dick Rutan and Space Ship One. Mojave was already advertising itself as 'Spaceport Mojave' on their 'welcome to town' signs.

After a while, good ol' doubting Clyde, who had once told me he had seen wind in the AV so strong that it could scoot an anvil along the ground, chimed in with a snort and said, "Well if they comin' to invade us we got nothing to worry about do we, if they can't tell the difference between Edwards California and Area 51 Nevada."

~ * ~

A bit later on when I was on my way home to Michele, I began thinking about the bar conversation. This was a dangerous thing. A couple of times before I had started thinking about bar conversations, and it had gotten Dave and me into some sticky situations. Of course Dave wasn't with me so I had no one to talk to about my thoughts and as I drew closer to home, I remembered that last time my thoughts had gotten Dave and me into trouble, Michele promised I could find someone else to go my bail next time an adventure ended badly, so I closed my thoughts up and did my best to forget about them.

A couple of days past and, try as I might, curiosity about Area 51 kept pricking my mind like a tiny hair splinter will prick your finger when you rub it just a certain way. But I didn't let the thoughts get out of hand like I had the wonderation about Disney, which had landed me and Big Dave and a couple of other people in the LA County Lock up for a couple of days. I am convinced the Universe or God or something has a great deal to say about these things because just when I thought I had gotten control of the Area 51 fever, Michele got a call from her sister. Now Michele's sister's life has been a soap opera ever since I have known her, but there had been a sudden up tick of the soap leaving Sis aground and in need of comfort, so Michele packed an overnight bag and headed for Simi with a simple, "I'll be back in a couple of days. Stay out of trouble." And she was gone. The vibration of the closing door had hardly stopped when the phone rang. It was Dave.

"Hey G," he said. "I just ran across an opportunity that you might like to get in on."

"Oh Yeah? What?"

"An outfit name of Willis Pictures is thinking about shooting a low budget sci-fi flick up in the desert near Area 51. I know all those guys and they asked me if I would go up there and scout some locations and shoot some pix around the area, so I said yeah. You wanna come?"

"How you gonna get there? I can't see myself riding bitch on your Harley all the way to Nevada."

He laughed. "Naw. Willis said I could take his car. Lincoln Town Car."

"Ugh, a barge."

"Yeah, but it's a comfortable barge and he's paying for the gas."

"Bar in the back?"

"Yeah, and air conditioning."

I rolled the situation around in my mind for a little while. It sounded really tempting and it made that "wonder" itch start to burn in my chest.

"Michele is out of town," I said. "Gone to her sister's..."

"Then what she doesn't know won't hurt her, or us."

I let that roll around in my mind for a while too and remembered. Maybe she didn't really mean she wouldn't go my bail if things went salty. I mean she said she loved me and we had been married for forty years. Besides, what could go wrong?

Later that afternoon Dave rolled up in front of the house in a dark green Lincoln land yacht and honked for me.

"Kinda late to be starting this isn't it?" I said as I got in.

"I guess, but I had the car and the cameras and the gas, and it just seemed like we needed to get on with it. It'll be cooler anyhow."

"I reckon. If it's too late when we get over there, I guess we can find a place to crash."

"Hell, big as this thing is we can crash right here in the car. You take the back seat and I'll take the front.

50

I glanced to the back seat and saw he was probably right. I'm sure there are whole Asian families that grow up with less space.

We drove along in silence for a while just watching the Joshua trees go by heading north-east up old US 395. We could have cut a more direct route across Death Valley but neither of us wanted to get stuck out there in the middle of the night. It was late October so we probably wouldn't have died of thirst but still...Death Valley. Instead we headed up toward Mono Lake where we could cut across through Tonopah and hit what was called, even on the maps, *the extra-terrestrial highway.*

"You know anything about this Area 51, Dave?

"Just what I've read and seen on TV."

"You figure there really are flying saucers and little green men up there?"

"I figure if there are they are in cahoots with Big Brother."

I thought about that for a little bit and had to shake my head. "David, I spent two years in the Army and twenty-two years dealing with the Air Force and other US of A government agencies and couldn't any of 'em keep a secret for shit. All you'd have to do is hang around some of the local watering holes for a couple of days and you'd know everything there was to know about everything happening on the base."

"That reminds me," Dave said. "You got your Military ID on you?"

"Always. Why?"

"Cause your card and my silver tongue are gonna get us on base to have a look around."

"I said you could find out anything by hanging around, but I doubt they are gonna just let us in the gate on the weight of my retired civilian dependent ID Card. They're stupid, not STUPID! If ya know what I mean."

"Reckon we'll find out," he said.

~ * ~

We spent the next several hours looking at the scenery and singing with the radio until it got pretty much too dark to see anything outside the headlights. By then we had crossed into Nevada and passed Tonopah and were looking for the turn off onto Nevada Highway 375. *The Extra Terrestrial Highway.* By then it was getting lateish and we were both getting tired and thirsty. We turned onto Highway 375 and started the final leg of the trip. The road was not promising as to lodging or food or drink. It was one of those *no-lights, total dark, more like driving down a long black tunnel* roads. Nothing seeable along the sides until there suddenly was something to see. The headlights washed over two guys beside the road with their thumbs stuck up.

Now myself, I had hitch-hiked a few thousand miles in the US when I was a kid. When we were stationed in Europe the whole family had hitched around in times we had no car, but not since. I have gotten a little older and gotten a little more cynical, or maybe scared. I couldn't remember the last time I hitched a ride, but more importantly I couldn't remember the last time I had picked up a hitchhiker.

The hitchhikers surprised Dave too, so much that he let out a big "Holy..." and whipped the car away toward the middle of the road while stomping on the brakes hard enough to squeal and smoke the tires.

By the time we got stopped, the two hitchhikers were standing beside the car. It takes a long time to stop a big old Lincoln Town car, but, now that I think about it, it still seems like they got to the car pretty fast, but anyhow there they were. A couple of Air Force guys, an A1C and a Senior Airman, in blues and fore and aft caps.

"You guys okay," they were asking, their voices muffled by the closed windows and the humming air conditioning. I rolled down my window, and they asked again if we were okay.

"You guys just scared the shit out of us, popping out of the dark like that. What the hell are you doing out here in the middle of nowhere?" I asked

"That's a long sad story I don't even want to go into," the Senior Airman said.

"Sounds like it involves women," Dave said.

The A1C let out a kind of pitiful groan, and the Senior said, "Please."

Dave and I both laughed. "Where you headed?" I asked.

"Back to the base, to lick our wounds in solitude," The senior said.

"Would that be Area 51 kinda base?" Dave asked.

"Yeah."

"You guys work over there?"

"Hey, then you are just the guys we'd like to talk to."

They both looked suspicious and said, "Uhm..."

Dave's words struck these guys almost like he had hit them with a shovel or something. They both hung their heads and shook them in gestures of negation. "More flying saucer chasers," the A1C said.

"Ah come on guys," I said. "We are just out here scouting locations for a movie..."

"A Zombie Movie," Dave said. "Zombies from outer space."

This was the first I had heard about Zombies so I figured Dave was making it up as he went along, but I was willing, so what the hell...

"Yeah," I said, "and since you guys are stationed around here I bet you know some great places for Zombie Massacres and stuff..."

"And we'd even buy ya a beer in return for the information," Dave said. "If there's any place to buy beer out here."

That seemed to perk them up some. "I could use a beer, for sure," the Senior said.

"Great," Dave said. "Where we going?"

"That way," the A1C said pointing up the road toward Area fifty one. "Only joint along here is the Space Ship Bar and Grill just outside the base gate."

Spaceship Bar and Grill? I thought, and the thought sent a shiver down my spine.

~ * ~

The joint was aptly named. It was a cinder block building which had a sheet metal facade over the front. Above the building was a long skinny antenna with a red ball on top, and over the entrance was a red and blue blinky sign that said SPACESHIP BAR AND GRILL.

The place wasn't exactly jumping. I didn't see another car in the dirt parking lot, and as I thought about it I didn't remember any cars passing us as we moved down the road. Area 51 was pretty much out in the toolies, but I figured a base as famous as Area 51 would at least have some traffic going in an out. It was pretty late, so I didn't think about it much. I was tired and thirsty and ready to curl up in the back seat of the land yacht and cop a couple of Z's.

We got out and headed up the ramp that looked like a big silver tongue lapping out of the front of the bar...and that is the last thing I remember, I mean really remember. I have some vague memories like the rags of a dream that didn't make any sense at all. Flash pictures of people leaning over me, but not exactly people. More like gray blobs with big black eyes and slit nostrils. I remember being cold because I seemed to be naked on some kind of a steel table.

Then it was morning. I woke up stretched out in the back seat of the Lincoln with what felt like the worst hangover I have ever endured. Throbbing head, throbbing nasty stomach, throbbing anal sphincter like I had just gone through a colonoscopy. I was almost afraid to move for fear something might fall off and bring on wider disaster.

"Dave," I said. It came out kind of a croak. My voice was rusty-crusty like after a lot of hollering at a ball game. I cleared my throat and tried again. "Dave."

"Whaaa?" he answered from the front seat.

"What happened?"

"Whaaa?"

"I am hung over like a big dog," I said. "Whad ya let me drink so much for?"

"Let ya drink? I don't remember drinking nothin.' "

A knock on the window scared us both. It was a couple of Air Force Security cops complete with gleaming bloused boots, blue berets and M16's. They weren't aimed at us but they were in a position where they could be without too much difficulty.

"Out of the car," one of 'em commanded.

I managed to sit up without my head exploding, but it was a near thing, and when I bent a little to pull up the lock knob on the door, there was a real danger of something else exploding, but I held it down thinking it probably wouldn't help my case any if I barfed on the cops' shiny boots.

Dave appeared to be having the same trouble which was why the cop could spin him around into the classic pat down position without resistance. I had never seen anybody manhandle Big Dave like that and I had always figured that if anyone tried it they were in for trouble. Like I said, Dave was mostly a gentle giant, but he had his limits.

My cop spun me around, and I just sorta naturally assumed the position leaning against the car. Now I've been frisked before, but it seemed like this guy was enjoying it more than he should have. I sure wasn't. The third time he bashed/squeezed my jewels I was considering swinging around and puking on those shiny boots just to get even.

By and bye the SP's seemed satisfied that we weren't armed so they spun us back around and asked, "What the hell are you people doing here?"

"We ain't doing anything officer," I started out. "Just sleeping in the car. That isn't against the law is it?"

"It is if you're sitting just outside the gate of a military facility," Dave's cop said. "Bomb's and terrorist attacks and stuff," he went on as though talking to a three year old.

"We got no bombs or bad intentions," Dave said. "We just stopped here to have a beer with a couple airmen we picked up hitchhiking."

"Stopped for a beer?" my cop said, doubt clear in his voice.

"Yeah," I said, a bit more crankily than I probably should have. "Just go in and ask the bar..." I hooked a thumb back over my shoulder at the SPACESHIP BAR AND GRILL, but as I did, I turned my head a little and noticed Dave was turned completely around and facing the bar with this astonished look on his face. I turned on around and probably got that same astonished look since there was no building or any sign that there had ever been a building there.

"There was a bar there last night, officer," I said. "Kind of a crappy looking place with a neon sign that said SPACE SHIP BAR AND GRILL. Even kinda looked like a flying saucer."

The SP didn't look convinced. He looked at his partner and at Dave who said, "Honest to God Officer, he's telling the truth. It was right there."

"Uh Huh," Dave's SP said, not sounding at all convinced. "Okay, turn around and put your hands behind you, both of you."

I glanced at the M16 and didn't even consider doing anything but what I was told. In moments we were hand cuffed and sitting in the back seat of a blue and white hummer.

"Boy I hope Michele was kidding about just leaving me sit in the slammer if I got sent there again," I whispered to Dave.

~ * ~

The SP's drove us past the gate guard shack and right onto the base. Area 51 was right in front of us, but there wasn't a whole lot to see. Just more desert. I figured the hangers and flight line were on the other side of a rise of hills that was just off to our left. We had wanted to get onto the base, well, we succeeded admirably, much to our dismay.

We followed the black topped road until we came to a small group of buildings. We still couldn't see the flight line, but we could see the big blue and white sign that said 96th Security Police Squadron. Our captors parked in front and marched us in the door and into a holding cell. They uncuffed us and went through the whole schmear of taking our belts and shoe-laces just to make sure we didn't do ourselves serious hurt and I thought about Arlo Guthrie and Alice's Restaurant.

Over the next several hours we were questioned by first a Master Sergeant, then a Captain and finally by a Colonel. We told them all the same story about coming to shoot location pix, and picking up the two hitchhiking Airmen, and stopping at the bar that was no longer there, and not remembering how we got back in the Lincoln or anything else until the SP's knocked on the window this morning. We swore repeatedly that we weren't UFO hunters or Area 51 watchers, but it didn't seem to do any good. Nobody believed us.

After hours of questions and answers, they delivered us some food and drink on stainless steel trays and that did not bode well.

"Good thing Michele is out of town," Dave said, "'Cause it looks like they are gonna keep us for the night anyhow."

"You got anyone you can call to get us out of here?"

"I got a lawyer friend but, in case you hadn't noticed, we haven't been offered our phone call. We are being held incommunicado, which is illegal, or was until 'Homeland Security' got power to tap phones without warrants and stuff. We may end up in Cuba for all I know."

I swallowed hard. "You don't really think they'd do that, do you?"

He shrugged. "Wouldn't think so, but as crazy as everything else has been, who knows?"

We sat and pretended to eat and thought our own thoughts for a while, then Dave asked, "What do you remember about last night?"

"Just what I been telling the cops. Same as you."

"Do you remember actually going into the bar, or whatever it was?"

I rolled that question around in my mind for a while before answering, "No. I remember getting out of the car and walking up that ramp thing that looked like a big tongue hanging out the front door but that is the last I really remember."

"Yeah, me too. Did you dream while we were asleep in the Lincoln?"

"Not really. Vague stuff. Big headed people with big black eyes and being cold and scared, but not able to really do anything about it."

"Me too. I'm beginning to wonder if maybe those Airmen we picked up weren't exactly what they seemed," Dave said with an ironic lift of an eyebrow.

~ * ~

By and bye they came and pulled us out of the holding cell and put us into a cell with bunks. That didn't make me feel any better, but at least they left us together. Now a steel box bunk is not comfortable at the best of times, but when you don't have the slightest idea what is gonna happen next, it is even more uncomfortable. Nevertheless, I managed to sleep a little and I guess Dave did too because we both had to be shaken awake in the morning.

Our alarm clock was a guy in a gray suit that looked as though he had slept in it. He needed a haircut and could have used a little mouthwash, but I remembered I was still in custody so I kept my mouth shut.

"Who are you?" Dave asked

"Bob Jones. I want to ask you a couple of questions."

"Go ask the SP's," Dave said. "They got all the answers we could give 'em, and I'm tired of repeating myself."

Brother Jones was sorta taken aback and glanced from Dave to me, but I had nothing to say so he turned and called out "Airman..."

A Uniformed Airman SP came and opened the cell door. Brother Jones said, "You guys want some coffee? Maybe some breakfast?" sounding very friendly.

Dave and I glanced at each other with a *what the hell?* kind of look, but we got up and followed Jones out and into what looked like a break room where steaming cups of coffee were already waiting for us.

We sat down and cautiously sipped the coffee, which wasn't awful.

"I know you guys have told your story a hundred times already," Jones began, "but if you'll humor me by telling it one last time maybe we can get you out of here and on your way again."

That sounded good to me, so I told him just what we had told everyone else.

When I shut up, Dave said, "Just who are you, Bob? Not Air Force I'd guess, and I'd bet my last nickel your name ain't Jones either, so just who are you? CIA? NSA? "

Jones lifted an eyebrow, no doubt considering whether to simply stick us back in our cell and leaving us to rot, but after a little he said, "I'm ETLO. Part of Project Blue Book."

"Blue Book?" I said. "I thought Blue Book was long gone."

"Only parts of it."

"You're here to find out if we were really kidnapped by little green men," Dave said.

"And to de-brief us about it."

Jones shrugged. "More or less."

"What does ETLO stand for?" I asked.

"Extra Terrestrial Liaison Office," he said. "Now, if I could have your version of what happened Mr. Dodge?"

~ * ~

Jones listened and questioned us for a couple more hours as we told basically the same story again. "Why do you think they chose you?" he asked.

"I think we just happened to come along," Dave said. "They were just like some naturalist out tagging wolves to study their hunting habits. They grabbed us because we came into their sights."

"Do you think they 'tagged' you?"

"Maybe. There have been reports of other people who have been 'taken' finding odd little metal pellets under their skin and stuff. They might have put some kind of device up my ass."

"Yeah," I added. "I sorta felt like I'd had a colonoscopy when I woke up."

Jones nodded. "Would you consider allowing us to fluoroscope you to see if they did tag you?" he asked.

Dave and I looked at one another, and finally Dave shrugged. "Sure, why not, so long as it gets us out of here."

~ * ~

After they X-rayed us, they turned the Lincoln and the cameras back over to us and escorted us out the same gate we had come in, making sure we didn't stray between the clinic and the front gate. We pulled into the lot where the SPACESHIP BAR AND GRILL had been, and the blue and white SP hummer pulled in right behind us.

"Okay, Now what, Dave?"

"Now we do what we came here to do, take location pix, starting with an open lot where a spaceship landed." He reached into the back seat and pulled up a camera then got out. I had my doubts that the SP's would let us take a picture so close to the gate, and when Dave got out with the camera the SP's, armed with their M-16's, got out and stood beside their hummer, but they didn't interfere as Dave shot several pix of the lot and the open desert around it. He did make sure not to aim at the cops or at the gate and when he was finished, he got back in the car as did the cops. "Okay," I said, and noticed I'd been holding my breath. "Can we go now?"

Dave grinned at me. "What'sa matter G? You nervous?"

"Nervous? BUGGER ALL! Nervous! Will you just drive already?"

He laughed and hit the gas, leaving the cops and their hummer in a cloud of dust.

I figured we were on our way back to Lancaster, but I was wrong. We got down the Extra Terrestrial Highway a few miles when Dave pulled to the side of the road. A dirt road led off into the desert toward a line of bluing hills in the distance. "What's up?" I asked.

"I promised Willis I'd shoot some pix and I'm gonna do it."

I got the distinct impression that there was more to it than that. "You really think that's a good idea in view of what we just went through?"

"Sure, what the hell? What else could happen?"

I shook my head and thought back to a lesson I learned so long ago I'd forgotten when. "David," I began, "never, ever, under any circumstance dare worse."

He studied me for a moment, but finally said, "Ahh. We're just gonna take some pix. That's all."

61

I didn't believe a word of it, but I was willing to back Dave up in about anything so I said, "Okay. Drive on." He narrowed his eyes quizzically at me again, but after a moment he completed the turn onto the dirt track and we were off.

Now I don't know that Dave was actually setting out to find the SPACESHIP BAR AND GRILL again, and if he had intended to find same, how the hell he accomplished it, but we had gone down that dusty desert track about five miles when I saw the sun glinting off something in the distance. That sun glare made my stomach turn over, but I kept my mouth shut telling myself that it couldn't possibly be what I was afraid it was. Dave didn't say anything, just kept driving and after a bit, there among the creosote and grease wood bushes was The SPACESHIP BAR AND GRILL, or at least the (a) spaceship that might once have been disguised as a bar. Now there was no blinky sign and no tongue-looking ramp flapped out the front. This was a largish silver disk, domed on top that was maybe forty feet tall and a hundred feet in diameter. It was sitting on three stubby legs like the legs on the bottom of an Aladdin lamp. It wasn't whirling or blinking or anything, it just sat there in the desert brush looking incongruous. No one was stirring around the disk, not even a mouse or a jack rabbit.

Dave stopped the land yacht right in the middle of the road, picked up the camera that had been sitting between us and rolled out his door. I wasn't convinced that was the best course of action, but like I said, I usually back Dave up in pretty much everything.

"Get the other camera, G," he said snapping pix of the saucer. I did as I was told and started shooting my own pix of the saucer and of Dave shooting pix and the land yacht all in the same frame.

After a few minutes of photography, Dave walked across the brushy space between the road and the saucer then stood there beside it with his hands on his hips glaring at it. At last he reached out and touched it, gingerly at first as though it might be hot or might give him a static electricity shock, but then he took the flat of his hand and smacked the smooth metallic surface hard. If it had been a bell, it would have rung from the slap, but as it was, the sound was more like a thud as if he had smacked his hand into concrete. He waited a moment and then did it again with the same result.

"Maybe there's a door bell." I said, taking another pic of him standing beside the saucer.

"If there is I don't see it," he said stepping back. He looked from the saucer to the ground around it and spotted a fair sized rock. He walked over and picked it up. It was a handful and looked like pink granite. He went back to where he was beside the saucer, drew back his arm and began pounding on the metallic side. He hit it a half dozen times before stopping to check if he had done any damage. He hadn't. The gleaming side looked as though it had just been polished without as much as a finger smudge on it. After a little, Dave set at pounding on the side of the ship again with what seemed a little more ire, but with the same result.

"I don't think there's anybody home, Dave."

"Bastards!" he said, and took to pounding on the side of the ship like a mad man.

I let him go at it for a little while but it was hot and I knew he couldn't keep at it long, so when he began to slow down, I stepped up and grabbed his wrist as he took another swing. "Forget it Dave. They ain't home or they ain't coming to the door, so forget it." He was dripping with sweat and breathing pretty hard. He'd really been laying into his shots. "Come on back to the car and let's get some water and some air conditioning," I said. I took the rock from him and dropped it on the ground then put my arm around his shoulders and led him back to the car.

We got in and started up the Lincoln to get the AC blowing and I got a couple of bottles of water out of the fridge in the rear. Turns out there were a couple of cans of Fosters Lager in there too, so I got them out as well.

Dave drank his bottle of water, and I drank mine then we popped the beers and took a sip. After a bit I asked, "you okay now?"

"Yeah, I suppose. Pisses me off though. Bastards kidnap us and stick things up my ass and then leave us to the cops like we were a couple of tagged coyotes without as much as a by your leave or a kiss my rosy ass, and now they won't even come out to apologize for all they trouble they caused us."

"Yeah, it is...perplexing."

"*Perplexing*," Dave snorted. "I'd say *perplexing*, just don't quite cover it. Why for a plug nickel I'd turn this damn Lincoln around and ram it right into that thing! Perplexing!"

They must have had some way of listening to what was going on in the Lincoln or maybe it was just coincidence, but Dave had no more than drawn another breath before there was a whirring sound that drew our attention back to the saucer and we saw a ramp coming down like a draw bridge from the side a little to the right of where Dave had been pounding with his rock.

Dave was out of the car and running toward the spaceship before I could hardly take it in, but when it did get through my neurons what he was doing, I rolled out and tried to catch him.

The ramp hit the ground about the time Dave got to the saucer and he had taken a couple of steps up toward the opening when the same two guys we picked up hitchhiking stepped out and started down. They weren't dressed as Airmen now. They were in jeans and tee shirts. Dave didn't even slow down. He opened his arms like a man about to make a tackle and hit both of the Airmen like a runaway truck. They all went down in a heap and after a moment Dave sorted it out enough that he was sitting on one guy's chest and holding the other one by the collar shaking him like a terrier shaking a rat.

Just as my foot hit the bottom of the ramp, a swarm of little gray guys with big heads and black bug eyes came pouring out of the door and covered Dave like ants swarming over a sugar cube. I wasn't exactly sure what to do, but when I reached the swarm, I piled in with both fists and both feet. Don't know that I did much good because there were a mess of 'em and the two humans managed to get loose and start fighting back, but I gave it all I had until something hit me like a lightning bolt and I lost consciousness.

~ * ~

I came to back in the cell where I had spent the previous night or one just like it. I was alone and felt like I had been worked over with a rubber hose, but I had some mad left from the fight, so when I managed to get myself out of the bunk I went and grabbed hold of the bars and started screaming for the jailer. It didn't take long for an SP to show up.

"Hey, shut up in there," he ordered.

"Let me outa here! I didn't do anything. Where's Dave? What the hell are you people doing?"

"Your friend is okay," the cop said. "He just hasn't come out of the zap they hit him with. Said it took three shots to knock him out. That is one strong SOB."

The guy that had called himself Bob Jones came in and said, "Thank you, Airman. I'll take care of Mr. Helm now."

The cop said, "Yes sir," and didn't salute, though he looked like he wanted to before he turned and went out.

"Where's Dave?" I demanded.

Jones didn't come too close, like he was afraid I was gonna reach through the bars and throttle him, which I might have if he had tempted me a little more. He said, "It's just like the Airman told you. He is just waking up. He's a little groggy."

"How the hell did I get back here?"

65

"Mr. Smith and Mr. Black brought you back after the melee at the ship."

"Smith and Black?"

"The guys you picked up the other night."

"Friends of yours are they?" I asked, beginning to put two and two together. "They work for Project Blue Book too?"

Jones didn't answer me, but he gave me a long speculative look. "Your friend is gonna be fine in a couple of hours and we'll have a little confab then try to figure out what we are gonna do with you two," he said shaking his head. He turned away, leaving me looking through the bars. I stared at the doorway he went out of for a while then I went and sat down on the bunk again, thinking that I was truly in deep shit this time. An agent of the US government had just told me they were figuring out what to do with me, so visions of lonely desert graves began to creep into my head, and then a vision of a small cell on a tropical island pushed that one out and I really started worrying. Nobody but Dave and my captors knew where I was. They could make me disappear like a fart in a hurricane and no one would be the wiser. That was when I started praying. "Oh Lord, if you get me out of this I won't ever do another stupid thing in my life."

I could only plead with God for so long before the other part of my mind began ticking over. Had Dave and I really been in a fight with little gray flying saucer men or had my cheese just slid off my cracker.

The promised two hours passed and then a couple more passed. I noticed that my Timex watch was stopped at two o'clock. So much for 'takes a licking...' Two M16 toting Airmen came in followed by Brother Jones. He held up a set of handcuffs, dangling them from an index finger. "You gonna be nice or do we need these?" he asked.

I took a deep breath and said, "I'll be nice," but I privately thought, *all depends on how things go.*

He unlocked the cell, and the Airmen fell in on either side of me, and we marched out with Jones in front. It occurred to me I could throw a choke hold on Jones and have him down on the floor before the guards could actually do anything, but I let the thought go. It wouldn't accomplish anything except maybe get me killed.

In the room where we had eaten breakfast the day before, Dave was sitting at the table with a cup of coffee in front of him. He looked a little the worse for wear. When we marched in, he popped to his feet with a, "You okay, G?"

"I'm alright. How about you? They said they had to hit you three times with that Taser thing."

He grinned, looking more wolfish than sheepish as he sat back down. I took the chair across the table from him, and a cup of coffee appeared in front of me which smelled wonderful. I picked it up and took a sip.

Jones sat down and the guards left the room. He looked from Dave to me and then back.

"What we oughta do is take you two idiots out in the desert and just shoot ya. It would make my life a hell of a lot easier. Why the hell didn't ya just go home?"

"If you and your little gray buddies had just let us be, we'd probably have done just that." Dave began. "But nobody sticks nothin' up my ass without my permission. It just ain't acceptable. I don't give a damn if they *are* from Alpha Centauri or where ever."

"You went looking for trouble!" Jones snapped.

"They started it," I said.

He held up his hands in, if not surrender then at least in acknowledgement.

An Airman came in carrying a stack of papers which he placed in front of Jones. He placed two ball points atop the stack then went out.

"Okay," Jones began. "What we gonna do is have you two sign some papers swearing you won't tell anyone anything about what has been going on here and then you are gonna get in your car and go away."

"I am signing nothing until I get some more information," Dave said.

"Me too," I added.

Jones looked from one to the other of us with a disgusted look on his face. "Are you guys crazy? This is all top secret and under the Homeland safety laws I could legally just pack you off to Guantanamo or some lesser known and not nearly as nice a place. I'm trying to do this without completely violating your constitutional rights."

"Seems to me like the Constitution got flushed a long time ago. When you let these little bastards trap innocent travelers for their experiments, that pretty well violated my rights," Dave said.

"Yeah, why did you let 'em do that, Bob?" I chimed in.

Jones seemed a little abashed and finally said, "I told 'em I didn't think it was a good idea, but the powers that be give these guys a pretty good bit of latitude. We owe them a lot and frankly, we're more than a little afraid of 'em. When they showed up in New Mexico back in '48, they made it clear they would and could make us hurt pretty bad if we didn't give back the pilot from that crash near Roswell."

"I thought that crash and stuff was all just urban legend," Dave said.

"So far as the rest of the world is concerned it is. There aren't too many people who know what really happened. Not even me, but I do know after that the little gray guys began coming and going pretty freely and people began getting picked up here and there for whatever the grays wanted. They promised not to really hurt anyone but they have traumatized a lot of people over the years."

"So all the flying saucer reports are true?" I asked.

Jones shrugged. "Some are, some aren't. Some really are just mass hysteria or hoaxes, but some are for real."

"How about all the 'Ancient Astronauts' stuff," Dave asked.

"I don't know. I am just a low level gopher working with the ETLO trying to keep the lid on all this mess, which brings me back to these non-disclosure agreements. If you'll just sign 'em and abide by 'em we can be done with all this crap and you can go home."

"And if not?" I asked.

"I wasn't kidding about Guantanamo. No signatures, you guys are on a transport out of here this afternoon to I don't *even* want to think about where, so maybe you oughta consider this for a little while."

~ * ~

Needless to say, we signed. They took all the pix out of the cameras and erased the memories and made sure we understood the threats they were making were not idle at all. On the way home Dave said, "Doesn't matter if we keep quiet or not anyway. They've done such a thorough job of discrediting all the UFO hunters and seers we wouldn't be believed anyhow."

"Still, they are gonna be watching us all the same," I said. "So we better keep our mouths shut."

Dave shrugged, "I guess. But how are they gonna know if we do talk? You think they have agents in the Windy City?"

"I think that after they fluoroscoped us, they didn't say if they found anything."

Dave's attention snapped to me. "You mean you think they really did tag us?"

"I'm saying that whether they did or not, I ain't gonna take the chance and tell anyone about anything that happened in Nevada."

After a little Dave said, "Yeah, I guess."

THE END

NO TIME LIKE THE PRESENT

"I got a chance to actually get a speaking part in a picture G. How 'bout that?" Big Dave said. He had been making some of his living as a movie extra for quite a while. He fit the part of "Hells Angel/crazy biker" perfectly in looks. Six feet six, two seventy or so with long hair and beard, which he sometimes braided like Black Beard the pirate. You've probably seen him, but didn't know it was Dave.

"Really? That'd be great," I said. "My buddy Big Dave is a movie star."

There were several other ears in the bar that turned to us when I said that. It was that kind of joint. A lot of actors and stuntmen and general movie hangers on. It was called 'The Second Reel' and was down on the wrong end of Sunset Blvd. near Vermont.

Lots of "Great for ya Dave" and "Hey, break a leg, Dave," but Dave didn't look all that happy about the whole thing.

"What's the pic?" I asked.

"B flick remake of 'The Time Machine.' "

"H.G. Wells. My man. I loved that book. You gonna play the Rod Taylor part?"

"Yeah, right," he sneered. "I'm probably gonna be a morloch."

"Morloch? They didn't say anything, just grunted and howled and stuff."

"Yeah well, it may wind up like that again. I said a 'chance' at a speaking part. Depends on a couple of things."

"Uh Oh."

"Yeah, Uh Oh."

"Whatdaya, gotta kill somebody or something?"

"No, but that would be easier I think. I gotta go talk Frankie Underdown out of his time machine."

"Who's Frankie Underdown when he is at home?"

"Ya know that junkyard looking place over at Hollywood Way and San Fernando Road in the Valley?"

"Looks like a fort?"

"That's the one. The Hollywood Trading Post."

"Geez Dave, do you know everybody in Hollywood?"

"Only if they are down and out or have something somebody wants."

"Uh huh."

"You know Frankie used to have one of the original King Kong dummies from the thirties production standing up there. Had to be thirty feet tall. Well, I don't guess it was Frankie who had it, he ain't that old, but it use to be there in the yard."

"Seems like I remember that from when I was a kid."

"Yeah. And he has got the Time machine from that Rod Taylor movie back in the sixties, which Bill Long, the producer of this dog, wants to use it in his flick."

"Okay. Can't he just rent it out or something? I mean…"

"Frankie wants about a million bucks to rent the damn thing, which tells me he doesn't really want to rent it out at all."

"Hum. How come?"

"More Hollywood legend stuff. The thing is supposed to be haunted or something."

This gave me pause. Big Dave Dodge and I have had some encounters with various dead and maybe undead people including Tiburcio Vasquez and Walt Disney, so when supernatural craziness and possible legal misadventure is mentioned, I always hark back to what my wife Michele told me the last time she got me out of jail. She said, "Next time you can find somebody else to go your bail."

"So, how you gonna talk this Underdown character out of his haunted time machine?"

Dave smiled a kind of wolfish smile and said, "I'm not gonna." He let me puzzle over that while he took a big sip of beer and then said, "You're gonna."

"Me? How I'm gonna…"

"Well it'll be easier than you think. Frankie is already a fan of yours. He's read a couple of your stories and he even bought one of your books…"

"Oh, he's the one huh," I said, cynically.

As Dave continued, "…And he plays guitar, which is a good thing since you were just bitchin' the other day about not having anyone to jam with anymore."

Now, ya gotta understand. I am one of those guys who has been lugging a guitar around since I was in high school. I'm pretty good, and I got a pretty good voice, enough that I even played some clubs when Michele and I were stationed in Europe, small clubs, okay converted gas stations, but I did play and I did get paid. I hadn't been playing much for quite a while because all my playing buddies were gone to other parts of the world or from this world, and the idea of jamming with someone again sorta tickled my curiosity. Besides which, if this Frankie was a fan of my writing, I owed it to him and to myself to show up and…

"Who you think you're kidding Dave," I grumped. "He prob'ly never heard of me and doesn't care a rat's ass about playing guitar."

"No," he protested and raised his hands like he was surrendering. "That was the honest to God truth. And I told him I'd bring you around to sign the book."

That gave me pause. "You sure you're not shittin' me?" I asked.

"Hand to God," he said. "Besides, you spin a pretty good yarn and I may need you to back me up."

"Oh Lord," I began. "Is this gonna get us in trouble again? I'd really like to stay out of jail and stay married a few more years anyhow."

"How can we get in trouble just talking to Frankie about borrowing his time machine?"

How indeed.

~ * ~

I picked Dave up the next afternoon in my little silver bullet of a car since his only transportation is his Harley, and I was not gonna ride bitch trying to carry a guitar case. We came down the 5 Freeway from Lancaster and got off at Hollywood Way in the Valley. Took about five minutes to get down to San Fernando Road to the Hollywood Trading Post. It still looked pretty much like a junkyard standing in the midst of some pretty raggedy old buildings. It had been there for a lot of years. I remembered it from when I was a kid. It was surrounded by what looked like an old west cavalry fort, but not one that would have done much good holding off the *hostiles,* as John Wayne called the Indians in a couple of movies.

I parked at the curb in front of the entry way and we went in, me carrying my guitar case, and Dave carrying a bottle of Jameson's. The office was a dusty rat's nest of papers and old furniture with a desk in one corner and some filing cabinets along the wall. The place was unoccupied.

"Heard we were coming and hit for the high country," I said.

"Nah, he's probably just in back. He lives here too. Got an apartment back there," Dave said, then shouted, "Hey Frankie, you got company."

A voice from somewhere far off hollered, "Come on back," and we went out through the other door which lead back into a dusty rat's nest of a warehouse stacked floor to ceiling with old furniture and Lord knows what all else. The light was dim and kinda gray. Place was a fire trap for sure, and I wondered if maybe this Underdown character wasn't just some kind of a crazy hoarder.

Dave seemed to know where he was going, so I just tagged along trying not to get myself or my guitar case tangled in the cobwebs that were everywhere. I was kinda ducking and turning and when Dave made a turn, I followed him around it and nearly messed my pants! There, hanging about head high, was this huge gorilla head. Must have been ten feet tall complete with evil red eyes and big teeth and a red tongue sorta hanging out of his mouth. It took me a second to catch my breath and catch on to the fact Dave knew about this thing, because he was laughing like a madman, and as I was standing, moving my jaw trying to find some curse word big enough for my pal, this other guy stepped out from behind a stack of what looked like old army trunks. He was laughing like a hyena too, which did not endear him to me.

When Dave and the other guy finally caught their breaths enough to talk, Dave said "G. Meet Frankie Underdown."

Underdown was a *'little fella.'* But you must take that advisedly. Dave is six-six and I am six-three. Frankie was about five ten both in height and circumference with flaming red hair and full, bushy beard. He was dressed in faded blue overalls of the gallus and bib pocket kind. He stuck out his paw and said, "G. I want ya to meet King Kong, or at least his head."

"Damn! You about scared me to death with that thing."

75

"Yeah, I'm sorry about that but it is just such a great artifact it seems like a waste not to use it."

"Well I gotta tell ya, it scared hell out of me. It is a lot scarier than that King Kong ride at Universal Studios."

"Yeah, when I rode that one I was really disappointed. Come on in. Let's crack that bottle of Jameson's." Underdown said.

After a couple more turns through the maze, where I looked around each corner before making the turn, we came into a wider open space that was walled in with boxes and stacks of furniture and books. Except that it wasn't as neatly organized, it reminded me of the big warehouse where the Ark of the Covenant ended up in that movie. Inside the makeshift room was a sitting area, with couch and comfortable chairs, a dining table, and a bed cut off from the room by a tri-fold screen but still visible. There was some counter space where Frankie had a Coleman Stove and a microwave. An Arrowhead bottled water dispenser sat beside an ancient refrigerator. Not quite camping out, but not that far from it.

Frankie got out three small Mason jars, blew the dust out of them, and Dave poured a healthy dollop of liquor into each. After we had all lifted our jars to one another and drunk, I asked, "Is old King Kong out there a piece of the old one that used to stand out in the lot?"

"Yeah. I brought him in here when I bought the place ten years ago. It was beginning to look pretty ragged out there and both the hands were gone anyhow, so I brought the head in and cleaned it up some. Thought maybe I could rent it out. And I have a couple time."

We sat and looked at each other for a couple of moments, nursing at our drinks. I waited for Dave to lead in any conversation about the time machine, but he just kept sipping his Jameson's and looking at me.

"Ol' Kong is really how come I bought this place," Underdown said. "I figured I owed it to him since he kept my brother out of Vietnam."

I rolled that statement over in my mind a few times, but finally had to say, "How's that again?"

Frankie laughed. "See back in '68 they were still drafting people. My brother Billy was nineteen and not in school and mostly just hanging around with a bunch of undesirables..." he looked at Dave and lifted his jar with a grin. "Anyhow, Billy decided that he didn't want to get drafted and maybe killed, so he came up with a plan. He knew convicted felons don't get drafted so he convinced a friend to help him steal one of King Kong's hands, so they broke in here, Kong was still standing out in the yard at the time, and cut off his right hand. They didn't try to hide it or anything. Took it to my Grandma's house over in Sun Valley and stuck it out of an air vent at the front of her garage. Folded the fingers up so that Kong was flipping the bird to everybody that came down the street." Frankie paused to laugh and shake his head. "You know it took the cops two full weeks to notice that gorilla finger. I think Billy finally had to call in an anonymous tip, but they finally came around to Momma Vella's house and arrested Billy. Tried him and found him guilty of grand theft gorilla fingers and sent him to jail for eighteen months." Now we were all laughing.

"So what did they do with the hand?" I asked.

"Brought it back here. Forty years later and I got it buried back in the warehouse somewhere. It's a raggedy mess, but it kept Billy out of the army so I couldn't just cut it up and throw it away. He'd kill me."

"That's a great story Frankie," I said. "You oughta write it up and maybe submit it to some producers or something. Dave could probably help ya with that. He seems to know everyone in Hollywood." I looked pointedly at Dave.

"You could write it up G," Underdown said. "You're pretty good. I give you my permission. If you sell it for a million bucks, you can give me ten percent."

That started my mind ticking over, but then I remembered why we were really there. "Maybe I'll do that," I said. "And maybe you can tell me the story about the haunted time machine. I betcha I can sell that one for sure."

Frankie looked from me to Dave and back again.

"Subtle G," Dave said. "Like hitting him with a hammer."

"Serves ya right for that King Kong stunt."

"Ah, relax Dave. I knew that was really why you were here." He turned to me and said, "But I really do want ya to sign your book. I really like it. The way it ended I'm thinking you maybe have more about the Design coming."

I felt my face getting a little hot. I don't do well with compliments. "Maybe," I said. "But it ain't like the thing topped out on the best seller list."

"Later maybe," he said with a big grin.

"Yeah, maybe. But now how about the haunted time machine. Dave is gonna have a heart attack if we don't get to that pretty soon."

Frankie looked from Dave back to me and back to Dave. "I don't know Dave, I'm telling ya…" he said

"Whatsa matter," I asked. "Is it really haunted?"

Underdown shook his head. "I don't think it is haunted as much as, I don't know, maybe cursed is a better word."

"Cursed?"

"Yeah. You know, bad juju and like that."

"Can we see it at least?" Dave asked.

Frankie was reluctant, but at last he said, "I reckon so if you must." He stood up then lifted his jar and took the last couple of drops of the Jameson's out of it, then he grabbed his guitar which was leaning beside the couch and said, "Bring yours too, G. You're gonna see something strange."

The whole idea struck me as strange, but like I said before, strange don't even begin to describe some of the places Dave and I have been, so I opened my case and took the guitar out and hung it across my back by the strap then we headed off down an aisle that was by Frankie's bed.

It was more of the same thing there as everywhere else in the place, cobwebs and dust and stacked junk. I noticed something else as we made our way along. There was a hum, not unpleasant, but persistent, that seemed to grow louder as we went along. I noticed the strings on my guitar were beginning to vibrate in sympathy with it.

At last we stepped from a narrow corridor out into a more open place and there it was, sitting right in the middle of the 'room,' the Time Machine from the '61 movie of the same name. The 'room' if you could call it that, seemed to be made of movers' quilts, folded and stacked higher than my head, and they surrounded the area where the time machine sat.

The thing wasn't very impressive. It looked like a big serving plate, maybe ten feet across, with another serving plate of about the same size set upright behind it. The painting was the most beautiful thing about it. All whorls and lines and hypnotic designs. The whole thing was set on a turn table, which made sense because they would want to be able to spin it around to shoot from different angles. There was a flat bench with a dash board kind of arrangement in front of it. The Dashboard had a mess of switches and some light fixtures, the kind that are red and green bulbs like operating lights to show if the thing is running or not. The hum was now so loud I could feel its vibration in my chest and my guitar strings were humming. I swiveled it off my back onto my front and set my arm on top so my hand hung down over the strings to stop them vibrating.

Around the time machine were three longish narrow tables with stuff stacked on them. As I approached, I saw the stuff was all religious material. Crucifixes, and Rosaries, and saint cards and a holy water bucket and sprinkler. On another was a chicken foot and a few amulets that looked like voodoo or Santa Rhea and a couple of carved African masks.

79

Draped over the dashboard part of it was something that looked like a Stoll from a priests robes. There were a half dozen folding chairs near the long tables.

We walked up to the thing, and Frankie took the sprinkle shaker out of the Holy Water Bucket and splashed a couple of drops onto the time machine, which gave me pause.

"Is that really holy water, Frankie?" I asked.

"Yep. I asked Father Mike from Holy Apostles for it and he obliged me. I asked him to come and do an exorcism on her too and he did," Underdown said sitting on one of the folding chairs.

We sat too.

"Exorcism?" Dave asked.

"Not like the movie. Priests do exorcisms all the time. When you move into a new house, you ask the priest to come and bless the place, and he prays and burns some incense and shakes a little holy water around. The point is to chase all the bad luck and such from the last tenants out of the house. No Demons or pea soup involved."

"So you had your priest do that to this thing?"

"Yep."

"Why?"

"Okay, let me tell you a story. While they were filming the movie, people began to notice the peculiar hum you're hearing. It wasn't too loud and it didn't cause problems really, but the sound techs played hob getting levels right and ultimately they ended up having to dub a lot of the dialogue after primary photography was done. Nobody thought much about it. They all just thought is was wind or some other kind of vibration in the studio. After the filming was done the studio carpenters were gonna just knock her apart and use the pieces for something else. I mean she is made of a couple sheets of plywood and some paint. But when they got ready to do it, it was like she knew. They couldn't get near her with hammers or crowbars. Everybody thought that was pretty weird but 'pretty weird' doesn't barely cause a ripple in Hollywood, so they just decided to put her in a warehouse and throw a tarp over her. Well, for some reason the warehouse developed a case of the shakes or something, and began falling apart. They got inspectors out there and checked it over and there were no termites or other causes, but it just kept falling apart and one day, a few years after the time machine had been stored there, it was like an earthquake came along one night and the whole damn place just shook to the ground. There was fire involved too, so the place was a total loss except for the time machine which didn't have as much as a scorch mark on it. They had inspectors climbing all over the ruins, but last I heard they said it was a 'localized earth tremor' followed by a broken gas line. Most everyone thought that was bullshit.

"Well, she passed through lots of other hands over the next several years and the destruction was anywhere from a little bit of cracked plaster to shaking buildings right off their foundations and that's how I wound up with her. I saw an ad that said, 'Original Time Machine from the '61 film of the same name for sale. Make offer.' So I went down to check it out and when I got there I noticed the hum. Even out in the open it gets you. They had it sitting outside in a big open lot and it had been rained on and sun damaged and all, so when I saw it I said, 'I don't want that thing, it's a raggedy piece of junk,' but I could feel that vibration right in my heart. It was like she was calling out to me to save her from the elements."

Dave and I had been exchanging glances since Frankie began his story and now our glances were of the, *this guy is spin-bug crazy,* type, but we didn't let on. Lots of people are crazier than Frankie and we still wanted to maybe borrow his time machine, but apparently Frankie had been more observant than we thought because he stopped, looked from Dave to me and back and said, "Yeah I'm nutty as hell to think she is alive, or sentient, or whatever, and maybe I am, but I'm tellin' ya there is something...she speaks to me. She sings to me. Listen."

He brought his guitar up from where he had left it leaning and strummed a nice rich E chord, then moved up to a B flat and on to a D. Classic blues progression then he sang out "*Hurry Sun Down, see what tomorrow will bring. Hurry Sun Down, See what tomorrow will bring. Well it may bring sunshine, and it may bring rain, yes it may bring rain.*" A classic, even ancient blues riff and as he sang the hum changed. It softened and sweetened somehow. It hadn't been harsh before, but now it was like a mother crooning to her child or a lover humming to the tune of her darling's breath. Warm and sensual and comforting, but exciting too.

Frankie finished his licks and looked at us out of the side of his eye. I noticed the hum was almost gone for a bit but it was building again.

"Go ahead G," Underdown said. "Try it."

I thought a moment and hit a C major chord and began singing, "*In the chilly hours and minutes of uncertainty I long to be, wrapped in the warm part of your lovin' mind...*" and it was like when Frankie was playing, only now that warm love seemed to focus on me. It was both sexual and maternal and was the strangest feeling I ever had in my life. At the end of the song, the hum from the time machine was barely audible, like the soft purr of a cat stroked into sleep.

"Oh that was good," Underdown said. "She really liked that."

"You keep saying 'she,' " Dave said. "Has she got some other name?"

"No, not that I know of. I mean she doesn't really speak to me or anything. I'm not sure she is 'alive' in the sense we think of as alive, but she sure as shit recognizes me and music."

"Charm's to sooth the savage breast," I said. "Or maybe beast, I can't ever remember, but there are a lot of things in this world that respond to music."

We sat in silence for a time listening and feeling the hum grow. It was like white noise, but far more sensual. At last Frankie began strumming and picking his guitar and sorta singing under his breath. I didn't recognize the song but I could feel the machine answering back.

Dave said, "You're never gonna let Long use this thing are you, Underdown." It wasn't a question.

Frankie stopped strumming for a moment and said, "Naw Dave, I don't think so. I think she's happy right here and I'm really afraid she might be dangerous out of my hands. I mean there's a long history of destruction with her."

"You could come along," I said. "Tend to her and keep her happy. Maybe this Long would even pay you scale to be a time machine wrangler or something."

Frankie was back to softly strumming. "I don't think so."

Dave waited for a few minutes before he said, "Okay Frankie, but think about it some will ya? We'll be back in a couple of days to find out if you changed your mind." He stood up and I followed.

Underdown nodded, but didn't stop strumming. "Can you guys find your way back out? I'm gonna stay here for a while."

"Sure, sure," Dave said. He gave me a head jerk to pull me along and we left. We could hear Frankie strumming for a long time.

When we passed back through the sitting room, we stopped long enough for me to put my guitar back in the case and I said, "You gonna grab the rest of that Jameson's?"

Dave shook his head. "Naw, leave it for Frankie. I think he may need it more than we do."

~ * ~

"No Benny, he isn't gonna let us have the thing for any amount of money," Dave said. We were sitting in a bar in Sun Valley called Skinny's, sipping at cold beer and Dave was on his cell. Personally, I hate cell phones. They could break into places like Skinny's and turn a perfectly good drinking establishment into a place of business, but it was modern Technology, both a blessing and a curse.

"I was just over there, Benny. He's convinced the thing is cursed or something and I gotta tell ya I'm about two thirds convinced myself."

He listened for a minute then said, "Okay, okay, I'll go try again." He listened once more. "Yeah I tried that. He didn't want anything to do with it, but maybe if you offer him a hundred K to be the wrangler, he'll budge. I don't think so but..."

The bartender looked toward us because Dave had gotten a little louder with each exchange, but I just smiled at him and lifted my empty glass in his direction.

Dave hung up and shook his head.

"Doesn't sound like brother Long knows how to take no for an answer."

"Yeah, but at least I got a money commitment from him this time. Maybe Frankie will go for it if he thinks he can get a hundred thousand out of it."

"I don't think so Dave. It's like he's in love with the damn thing."

"Yeah. It was pretty strange."

The bartender brought a couple more beers and we sat in silence for a time as we sipped them. At last I said, "We gonna go back and try again?"

"I'm tempted to just tell Long I went and he still said no, and let the whole damn thing go."

"Yeah, but then you won't get your speaking part..."

"And the film prob'ly won't get made at all."

"So drink up and let's go give it another shot."

"Yeah, okay," he said and slugged down the last swig of his beer.

We weren't far from the Hollywood Trading Post so it took us about five minutes to go back there. I parked in the same place and we headed in. I left my guitar in the back seat. Inside, Dave hollered like he had before and we started down the aisle toward Frankie's sitting room.

Of course I knew what was coming, but I still nearly scared myself to death rounding the corner right into King Kong's glare, but we didn't stop to laugh or swear this time, just kept going to the sitting room. No Frankie. Dave hollered again and still got no response.

"Maybe he's still down with the time machine," I said. "He hasn't been back up here 'cause that Jameson's bottle is right where we left it."

Dave looked at me and I could see the wheels of his mind turning, then, without another word he headed out toward the room where the time machine was. I followed him, getting a bad feeling in my stomach.

I noticed as we went along the aisles that, unlike before the hum was almost gone. I could hear it, but not like before when it was like a drill that went into your chest. *He must be singing to it,* I thought. *That's what got it quiet before.*

We reached the room and there was Frankie, only he was no longer sitting in the folding chair where we had left him. He was now sitting on the bench before the dashboard of the thing and the bubble lights on the board were flashing a steady walk time blues rhythm. He had his guitar on his lap and he was strumming it, but I couldn't hear any music. It was like the time machine was absorbing it all or something. "Hey Frankie," Dave hollered. "What you doing up there?"

Frankie didn't answer. Maybe he didn't hear. "Hey Frankie!" I hollered and Dave did the same right behind me but Frankie didn't budge.

We walked on up to the tables around the thing, and hollered again but to no avail. I pulled the holy water sprinkler out of the bucket and flicked a small shower at Frankie, but none of it ever reached him. The water sizzled like I had thrown it against a hot skillet. Dave looked at me then took the sprinkler and dipped it in the bucket and flicked it at Frankie with the same result.

"This is bad, G. We gotta get him out of there. I don't know what is happening but we gotta get him out of there."

I gave a nod and we stepped past the tables, only to run into the same hot invisible wall that vaporized the water. It was like a blast from an oven and it drove us back.

We looked at Frankie who didn't seem to have noticed us and then I began waving my arms to try to get his attention, but he just kept strumming his guitar and I could see his mouth moving, so he must have been singing, but we couldn't hear anything.

"Go get your Guitar, G," Dave said, and without really thinking about it, I took off back the way we came in.

I reached the sitting room quickly and ran on down the aisle I thought would lead back to the office and out to the car, but I was wrong, and in a few steps I was lost in the maze and turned around so that I couldn't tell which way was out. I stopped dead and turned around slowly, until I saw King Kong's head hanging down from the rafters. I headed up an aisle that seemed to be the right direction and in a couple of minutes I was gratefully looking at Ol' Kong's ugly face. I made it on out to the office and out to the street in a couple more minutes and got my guitar case out of the back seat.

I didn't get lost on the way back and when I reached the time machine room, I found Dave with a long pole, like the kind one uses to open high windows. It was maybe eight feet long and had a brass hook at one end. He was poking it at Frankie but was not having much luck. The pole seemed to sorta bounce off whatever the hot invisible field around the time machine was. Frankie still didn't seem to notice that we were there. He just kept strumming and singing.

"G. Get that guitar out and start playing."

"Playing?"

"I'm hoping you playing and singing will distract the machine so I can poke Frankie and wake him up or something."

Sounded more than a little desperate to me but I didn't have any better idea, so I swiped the cobwebs that had brushed off on the case as I ran down the hall and opened it up. I pulled the guitar out and dropped the strap over my shoulder and pulled the pick from where I had woven it into the strings. And that was it. I had no idea what to sing or even how to strum this guitar I had owned for twenty years.

"Play already!" Dave shouted.

"What? What shall I play?"

Dave looked at me for a second then opened his mouth and began to sing, "*Amazing Grace, how sweet the sound, that saved a wretch like me, I once was lost....*"A beautifully smooth baritone.

I joined in strumming as loud as I could and singing at the top of my lungs. "*...I once was lost but now I'm found, was blind but now I see.*"

I couldn't remember the next verse, so I went back and repeated the first verse and Dave followed me, all the time trying to poke through the heated shield with his window pole.

I felt the attention of the time machine turn a little toward me. I felt it in my chest like I had felt it before. Like a pulling at my heart. A pulling like I remembered feeling for Michele when we were young. This thing wanted me, wanted to embrace me like it embraced Frankie. It was love, or maybe lust, I don't know, I just know that I felt a sweet tugging at my heart and in my head, and all of sudden I felt Dave smack me across the back of the head. I had walked up to him without even knowing I was moving.

"G! Stop. Wake up. Play!" He hollered at me. I came back to myself and began playing again. More hymns. They were all I could think of! "Old rugged cross" and "Shall we gather at the River" and the Martin Luther favorite "A mighty Fortress is Our God." That one seemed to doubly distract the time machine. And Dave managed to shove his window pole through the barrier and poke Frankie in the ribs. Frankie stopped strumming and turned his head, looking surprised but not inclined to move. Dave poked him again and twisted the hook end of the pole into the side of Frankie's overalls. He began pulling the pole back to himself hand over hand and Frankie didn't resist, but he didn't help either.

The pole was smoking now, just this side of bursting into flame. Dave and I were both sweating like stokers in a boiler room.

I finished all I could remember of 'A Mighty Fortress,' and saw that Dave was not making much headway pulling Frankie out, so I swung my guitar onto my back by the strap and grabbed onto the pole to help him pull. We went back to singing *Amazing Grace* and heaving on that pole with all of our might.

We pulled Frankie to the edge of the Time Machine platform then with one huge heave, we dragged him through the heat shield. It just took a second for him to cross the barrier, but the heat was so intense that his overalls began to smoke and his red hair and beard burst into flame. Dave began trying to pat the flames out with his hands, but I grabbed the holy water bucket and dumped it over Frankie's head.

Having Frankie pulled out of its clutches did not make the Time Machine happy. The sound that had been there before returned, only now it was more like a scream than a hum and the heat that had been radiating from it intensified. I could feel it burning my face and arms.

"We gotta get out of here!" Dave hollered.

The movers' blankets Frankie had stacked to help muffle the sound began to smoke and in a moment they began to flame. We turned and ran. Frankie was in a total daze and ran only because the fire was licking at our rear ends, and the scream from the Time Machine was following us. We didn't stop until we were outside.

Smoke was already rising in a black column and we could all feel the ground trembling under our feet. Dave got on his cell phone and called 911 but he apparently wasn't the first because he was still talking to the 911 operator when the first fire engine rolled up, siren screaming. I pulled my guitar off my back, threw it in the back seat of the silver bullet then jumped in and whipped a U turn right across San Fernando Road to park on the other side out of harm's way.

Frankie, Dave and I got out of the firefighters way, but there was not much they could do. The Hollywood Trading Post burned like a fuse, and I remembered all the dust and cobwebs and paper boxes. We were lucky to get out of there. But I also thought about the Time Machine. If the legend was true, it had been in another fire and not been hurt. Was it going to come through this one too?

The fire department wouldn't let us back into the place the rest of the day even though the fire appeared to be out. Next morning bright and early, the three of us picked our way through the ashes to where the Time Machine had stood. I don't know what we expected to find, but what we found was a circle a bit larger than the base of the Time Machine that was completely clean of ash and charcoal, as though someone had marked it with a compass and swept it clean right down to the concrete. There was no hum, no heat, no heart tug. It was just gone.

"There goes my speaking part," Dave said, shaking his head.

"Ah well. Maybe next time," I said.

THE END

TIME FLIES WHEN YOU'RE HAVING FUN

Big Dave and I were sitting in the Windy City Saloon one evening talking about going fishing. We both liked fishing and there were several places around the Antelope Valley where we could go to wet a hook.

"Pyramid Lake is good," Dave said. "It's real deep and cold. Lots of California Golden Trout in there." He flapped his hand at a couple of house flies that buzzed around us.

"Yeah and not too many boats." Now I flapped my hand as the flies had decided to come and buzz around my head. "Or we could try Lake Elizabeth."

Dave cocked an eye over the top of his beer glass and said, "I don't know about that one. Supposed to be a monster lives in that lake."

Anyone else might have thought Dave was just kidding about the Lake Elizabeth monster, but he and I had had some pretty strange experiences with what might have been ghosts or curses or UFO's, so we always considered local legend in making our plans.

"Yeah, ol' Lake Elizabeth is supposed to have a crack in the bottom that goes right down to hell. It's kinda nasty looking too. Water's real green and thick looking."

"That may be closer to the truth than you guys know," Clyde, another regular in the joint said. "Elizabeth Lake sits right on top of the San Andreas fault, so it really might have a crack that goes right to hell's door."

"Yeah, but there ain't no monster. One of the old timers that owned land around there got tired of losing his cows and sheep to the damn thing, so he waited by the lake one night until it came out to hunt then he emptied his Winchester into it and knocked it down. Didn't kill it though, so he jumped on it and pounded hell out of it till it got away. It took off headed east and ain't been around since. Supposedly it flew all the way to Arizona before it finally conked out. Tombstone Epitaph news paper ran a picture of it like it was a dead gun fighter or something."

The flies in the bar seemed to be multiplying and they all seemed to like Dave and me. We both were waving our hands around trying to keep the little beggars from landing in our beer.

"Jimmy," Dave called, "you got a fly swatter? We're about to get carried off over here."

Jimmy, the owner of the Windy City, came out from behind the bar with his swatter in hand. "If you guys would bathe more'n once a month you wouldn't have this trouble," he said and smacked a couple that had been foolish enough to actually land on the table.

"Why Jimmy, I'm gonna quit coming in here if you keep insulting me like that," I said. He laughed. "I ain't worried. Ain't another bar in the Antelope Valley that'll let you two in." He smashed a couple more flies then handed the swatter to Dave. "Here, maybe you can protect yourself with that." Then he went back behind the bar and started washing glasses.

At the right time of year, in the spring, the flies that plague the Mojave are the politest flies in the world. They buzz around in swarmy circles but they don't ever land on anything, but in the depths of the summer they turn into the most pestiferous, impolite beasts in the world. They land on anything living and just will not be shoo'd away. Sometimes you actually have to scrape

92

them off with the side of your hand to get 'em to move. There're horse flies mixed in with the blue bottles and houseflies, and they bite hard enough to bring blood.

We kept waving and shooing and swatting, and were busy enough that we didn't notice when another fellow came in the door. He went to the bar and claimed the stool next to Clyde. "G'day Jimmy, Clyde," he said in a faint Australian accent. "Give us a beer, will ya?"

"How ya doing, Croc?" Clyde asked. He had started calling the Australian 'Croc' after the Crocodile Dundee movies, and it caught on. It didn't seem to bother the Australian and he did sorta look like Paul Hogan. Skinny, dirty blond hair and a tan like he'd been working in the outback. All he needed was the hat and that big-ass knife.

Croc glanced over at Dave and me sitting at our table, waving our arms and the fly swatter. "What are you two doing, playing windmill?"

"Fly chasing," I mumbled.

Jimmy had set a beer in front of him and he took time to take a big swallow before saying, "You ain't ever seen flies like we got in Australia. They come in swarms of millions. Just cover a fella up like he was a pile of shit on the ground. That's why most Australians wear long sleeves, so the flies can't get to yer skin. They'll bite ya bloody."

"I've heard that," Dave said.

"I heard Australia didn't have many insects, especially flies, until the Brits brought cattle," I said.

"That's true," Croc said. "Just like with the rabbits. They didn't have enough natural enemies to keep the population down. Same with flies. They're a plague that just seems to get worse every year. Gotten so bad in the Northern Territories they're threatening the crocodile population."

Now every ear in the bar turned to him. We had all heard and told some of the most colossal lies imaginable but this sounded like a whopper to beat all whoppers.

"Threatening the Crocodile population?" Dave asked. "Pretty tough flies if they eat crocodiles."

Croc looked around the bar as if in astonishment. After a moment, he said, "No ya stupid git, they don't eat crocodiles. They eat things that crocodiles eat and the crocs are starvin.' Now as I think about it, they do sorta eat crocs too. They sometimes swarm the little fellers, especially their eyes and they sting and lay eggs in their eyes. When the maggots hatch out it blinds the baby crocs so they end up dead and the maggots eat 'em until they hatch out into full grown flies."

"Whew, that's pretty tough alright," I said. "I thought the crocs ate mostly fish."

"Yeah mostly, but a lot of the fish are the kind that feed off bugs and stuff that falls in the water and when the fish rise to get their dinner, the flies swarm them just like they swarm baby crocs. Lay eggs in their eyes and gills which kills 'em."

Dave and I waved and swatted a little more and then Dave said, "I was reading the other day that there were some special flies in Australia, other than just the usual house and horse and blue bottles."

Croc shot us a glance from the side of his eye and said, "Oh yeah, and what would those be?"

"Time flies," Dave said.

Croc gave us his full attention with that, but didn't say anything, so Dave went on, "Supposedly some native medicine man, whatever they call 'em, created these time flies to punish the white men who had invaded aboriginal lands."

"Sounds like a joke to me," Croc said and turned back to his beer, but there was something in his voice that made me sharpen my ears. "Time flies when yer having fun, and such as that." His accent had suddenly gotten a good deal thicker.

"Yeah, maybe. It was a pretty wild story anyhow. Something about how these magical time flies would bite a fella and he would get bounced

94

back in time, how far depended on how hard the bite was. Made the people who had been transported really crazy. They'd be almost at the end of their sentence and then get bitten by a time fly and find themselves backed up a couple of years."

"Yeah, pretty wild," Croc said and drained his glass. Jimmy picked up the empty glass and tilted it toward Croc, asking if he wanted another, but the Aussie shook his head, said a quick good bye and blew out of the place like he'd seen his ex-wife.

"Wonder what got into him?" Dave said.

~ * ~

I like fishing. I like sitting on the bank with my line in the water and a cooler full of cold beer beside me. But there are some things about fishing I don't like, such as getting up early, so I mostly don't. I'm not one of those big game fishermen that gotta use a fly reel and hike a hundred miles back into the wilderness to some trout stream. I like lake fishing with worms and salmon eggs and other bait. Dave was pretty much like me. Fishing was more just an excuse to sit in the quiet shade and BS and drink beer and maybe catch a fish once in a while, but that wasn't all that important.

Anyhow, Dave and I pulled into a big parking lot kind of a place beside Pyramid Lake. Down at the water side was a place you could launch your boat if you had one or rent a boat if ya wanted, but we didn't want a boat. What we wanted was bait and the boat rental guy sold bait and beer and tackle of all sorts, even sold sandwiches if you weren't too particular how old they were.

Inside the store, which was a shack built on a couple of pontoons floating beside the boat rental dock, we said howdy to the old man behind the counter. He was a cliché, beard, squinty eyes, leathery tan, with a beat-up cap that had a 'Bass Pro' patch on it and a checked shirt.

"Kinda quiet ain't it," I said. I mean it was a Wednesday morning, but I figured there would be at least a couple of loafers trying their luck, but when we parked the silver bullet, I noticed we were it. Not another car or a sign of another soul.

"Yeah. Quiet. What can I get ya?" he said.

Dave and I discussed it earlier and decided we needed some night crawlers, big fat juicy ones, some regular red worms, and two jars of salmon eggs, one red and one pink. We talked about meal worms, but decided if the bass were gonna bite they would bite red worms as well as meal worms so we told the guy, and he turned and pulled the paper cups of worms out of the cooler behind the counter. The salmon eggs were right there on the counter, so we just set the two jars beside the cups of worms.

The proprietor rang up the sale. I kept from calling him a thieving SOB when I saw the total, but just barely. Dave and I each threw in half the cost and after the money was safely locked up in the cash drawer the old man said, "Hope you catch something."

That was not the way it usually came out. People usually just said "Good Luck" or some such but there was something in the way the old man said "Hope ya catch something."

Dave and I glanced at each other, and Dave asked, "Where they biting?"

The old man hesitated but finally said, "Oh, here and there. Mostly they ain't been biting for a couple of weeks."

"How come?" I asked.

He shrugged. "Don't know, but I ain't seen anything bigger than a little old blue gill come out this lake for weeks, and not too many of them."

"Looks like we picked a great place to wet a hook, G," Dave said.

"Ah well." I kinda laughed. "Story of my life. My dad used to say, 'fisherman's luck. A wet ass and hungry guts.' "

Dave chuckled too. The old man didn't. We picked up our cartons of worms and jars of salmon eggs and went on out. We pulled the poles and tackle box and beer cooler out of the car, and walked on down to the lake edge. There was a pretty big old willow tree that grew right by the water and was usually a good place to catch blue gill if nothing else. It wasn't too far from the boathouse but far enough so should anybody come along and want to rent a motor boat, they wouldn't bother us with the noise or the ripping up and down the lake scaring away the fish.

Pyramid Lake wasn't a natural lake. It was a California Conservation Lake that was there to help control flood water that sometimes roared down out of the San Gabriel Mountains, and to conserve that water to use for farm irrigation. Incidentally it was made into a *recreational area* stocked with California golden trout and some bass and blue gill and crappy so the state of California could collect the fee for a fishing license from sport fishermen like me and Dave.

We sat down in the shade and baited up. Dave with red worms, me with night crawlers, and flipped our lines out. We got comfortable sitting there in the shade and popped a couple of Foster's lagers. There was a slight breeze which kept it cool but more important it kept the flies at bay, though just barely. There seemed to be a pretty big swarm of them around the willow tree. The lake was calm, not even ruffled by the breeze and there was something strange in that, but I couldn't quite put my finger on it.

"Old man wan't much encouraging was he?" I said.

"He didn't have to be with the prices he charged for worms and stuff."

"Yeah we probably shoulda just gone and dug up my backyard for the worms but, what the hell…" Something hit my line and I started really paying attention, but there was no more tug or bump.

"Probably just some little bait stealers," Dave said, meaning tiny minnows that would grow into bass or trout or whatever if they lived long enough.

"Yeah probably," I agreed and reeled in my line to find that whatever it was had indeed snatched my night crawler. I dug out another one and decided that since these worms were pretty much golden, I'd only use half. I pinched him in two, dropped half back in the dirt filled cup and put the other half on my line then flipped my line back out in the water.

The sound of a car coming onto the lakeside made us look up.

"Looks like we ain't gonna be alone after all," Dave said.

"Another loafer. Makes me not feel quite so much like a bum."

Dave laughed.

The car was an older model Land Rover that might have been silver once but now was so dirty it was more leaden gray than silver. We were surprised when we saw the driver was Croc the Australian. He rolled out of the driver's seat and came walking toward us. He didn't have a rod or tackle box and he seemed to be coming with purpose.

About then my line jerked again and I started paying attention, but just like last time I got one little jerky nibble and that was all. I began reeling in to check if the bait stealer had gotten my worm about the time Croc reached us.

"G'day Fellas," he said. "Catching anything?"

"Not so far, but we just got here. Where's your tackle? Join us. Want a beer?" Dave said.

"Yeah, I'll take a beer, but I'm not here to fish exactly. I need to talk to you fellas about something you said the other night."

Suddenly out of nowhere a gull swooped down. He was way inland but sometimes if the wind is right they get blown in and they seek out lakes to fish in. Gulls are nasty birds that are a botheration at the best of times, and now we had one in addition to the flies.

"What did we say," Dave asked. "Barroom conversation usually drifts around so much we could have been talking about anything."

"You mentioned Time Flies."

"That was supposed to be a kind of a joke, Croc. You know, *time flies when you're having fun.*"

"You were pretty specific about them though," he said. "About how getting bitten by a time fly could bounce a fella around in time."

The gull swooped low over the water a hundred yards out then rose and turned in the air.

"Yeah," Dave said. "I read something about such things in *Weird Tales of Science*. But that's just a Science Fiction mag so I figured they were from the fertile imagination of some scribbler like G."

The gull swooped again, a bit lower this time and as he hit the bottom of his swoop, the most astounding thing I ever saw happened. Up out of the lake a big fish, or I guess it was a fish, leapt up and snatched that gull out of the air as neat as you please and was gone with the bird in its jaws in a few seconds.

"Did you see that, Dave? Croc?"

"G, I think we may be using the wrong bait," Dave said.

~ * ~

"What the hell was that thing" I asked, more talking to myself than really asking. It was huge and strange, sorta like a big bass only the side fins were long enough that it looked like it could fly if it got turned just right into the wind.

"He's a victim of one of those Time Flies you were talking about, Dave," Croc said,

"You mean there really is such a thing?"

"Well, not exactly like you said. They aren't really flies and they weren't created, at least we don't think they were created, by Abbo magic.

What they seem to be is continuum anomalies. Little pin holes in time and maybe pin holes between dimensions. They were identified down under at first, but they seem to be all over the world. "

"I take it that means you aren't just an Aussie immigrant," Dave said.

Croc grinned and shrugged. "Not exactly. You might say I'm a 'Time Fly' swatter. I work for the Australian Science Commission Special Office. I travel round the world chasing rumors of strange things.

"Like giant flying bass that eat sea gulls," I said.

He shrugged again. "Among other things," He said.

"Other things?" Dave and I said together.

"Sure. Big-foot, and Nessie and the Lake Champlain sea monster. Other things not so famous."

I laughed, I couldn't help it. "You're a big-foot hunter?"

"Did you or did you not just see a fish big as a Land Rover snatch a gull out of the air?"

I stopped laughing.

"What do you do about these things when you find 'em?" Dave, always a practical man, asked.

"Depends. Nessie, we just left alone. She's hiding well enough and would have made quite a stir if we'd captured her for study, or killed her. Sasquatch, for all we could figure out, was just an Indian legend. Might have been real once, but so long ago that he probably died of old age. Now this fella here," he nodded at the lake. "Him I'm gonna try to catch and send down to Scripps in San Diego for examination."

"Won't that kinda let the cat outa the bag?" I asked.

"Eh, not so much. Oceans are full of strange creatures that never been seen up close."

"No way to figure out where they came from and send 'em back, huh?" Dave asked.

"Oh god! Bloody British TV! There are no sparkly anomalies that open and close to different times being kept secret by the British government. These things are more like nicks in the membrane between worlds that heal like a nick in your skin."

"Sorry," Dave said. "Just trying to get my head around this. It isn't like I got a hell of a lot to go on here."

"What causes these nicks?" I asked.

"Now that is the two bob question. No one has been able to figure out what causes it. If we knew, we might be able to do something about it."

"You said you're the 'Time Fly swatter'. Why are they called 'Time Flies' if they really have nothing to do with flies?"

"It started out as sort of a joke. It seemed like every time there was a break between dimensions there was a period when there were great swarms of flies hanging around the place where the break occurred. Someone suggested the flies gathered because the breaks were really inter-dimensional farts that the flies could smell, and then someone else did the same gag as you with 'time flies when you're having fun,' and it just sort of stuck."

"So it doesn't really have anything to do with flies?"

"Inter-dimensional farts," I said and laughed

"Disappointing," Dave said.

We chuckled for a good while as we finished our beer and looked out over the lake. Nice day. Lake was smooth as glass without so much as a ripple. That's when it dawned on me what had felt wrong all along. There were no coots, the little diving ducks that seem to flock to all of Southern California's lakes. The monster, or whatever you want to call it, must have eaten all the coots, and maybe all the fish big enough to make a bite.

"So how we gonna catch this beastie, Croc?" Dave said.

Croc looked us both over without saying anything, obviously considering, for quite a while before saying, "Well, I've got a couple of ideas."

~ * ~

Croc began trying to explain how we were gonna go trolling for the monster. "I've been down here observing several times," he began. "I think I know how to do this. We're gonna rent a boat and motor. I've got tackle in the back of my Rover to fix it up. You fellas go rent the boat and I'll hook up my tackle. I'm pretty sure the old man knows there's something going on but don't tell him any more than you have to."

I looked at Dave and he looked back. We hadn't exactly come heavily weighed down with money. We were just gonna drink some beer and maybe catch a fish, but if we wanted in on this little adventure we were gonna have to ante up.

"I think maybe he'll take a credit card," I said as Dave and I rolled up line and put lids back on our expensive worms.

"I'll help ya pay for it, G, when I get my money from Warner Brothers."

I knew Dave had money coming from a 'crazy wild motorcycle' bit he'd done in some movie, but Lord only knew when it would actually come through. Still, "Okay," I said with some trepidation. Any time I find myself in a dubious situation I remember times past wherein I had landed in trouble one way or another. I didn't see how this could be more than a small jam, but you never can tell.

Back in the bait shop, the old man looked at us funny when we asked for a boat and motor but he didn't say anything about it. Just wrote up the paper work. I showed him my California Driver's license and my MasterCard and he seemed satisfied. I sorta mumbled something about taking the boat over to the cliffs on the other side of the lake 'cause the fish weren't biting over here. The old man just looked me up and down and didn't say a word, just marched out to the floating dock to one of the aluminum john boats that were tied up there. He had to open another locked shed where he had a dozen or so small outboard motors hung up on a rack that looked like a long horse-hitching rail. He pulled a little Evinrude ten horse motor off the rack and said, "Grab a gas tank from over yonder." He lifted his chin at a line of red pump up gas tanks with black hose wrapped around the handle. "Be sure it's a full one," he said, and lifted up the little engine and lugged it toward the boat. I started to pick up the gas tank, but Dave beat me to it. I was kinda glad because I knew the tank full of gas was gonna be heavy.

I did as I was told and the old man set the steering fin of the motor on the dock, pivoted himself around the motor and stepped down into the boat, then lifted the motor, turned and in almost one fluid motion, set the propeller into the water and hooked the clamps onto the back center board of the boat. It occurred to me then that this old man might not be as old as he looked and old or not, he still had a plenty strong back. He screwed the thumb bolts down tight then took the big red gas tank from Dave and placed it in the rear of the boat. He loosened the thumb pump knob and pumped it a couple of times until a little bit of gasoline squirted out of the fixture at the end of the black hose then he plugged the fixture into the engine and tightened the pump knob again. "It ain't hard to start," he said, putting the gear lever into neutral, "but ya gotta prime it a little when it's cold." With that he pulled the start cord slowly out and let it go back, then he gave it a hard yank. The motor coughed and sputtered then caught and revved perfectly. He climbed out of the boat. "Be careful you don't flood it trying to start it next time. If it don't catch in a pull or two, just sit down and be patient for a little before you pull it again. Worse come to worse, there's a pair of oars in there."

Dave and I stepped into the boat and sat down. "Thank you," we both told the old man as he untied the rope and gave us a little shove away from the dock.

"Be back before dark," the old man said, "Or I'll have to charge you for two days."

"Yes Sir," I said aloud and waved back at him, "We oughta have our limit before then," I said so only Dave could hear me.

~ * ~

Croc was waiting back at the willow tree when we putt-putted up in our little boat. He didn't look all that impressed. "Coulda used one with a bigger motor," he said.

"This is all he's got. If it ain't big enough to suit you, we'll take it back and all go home," I said.

"Naw, it'll probably work. We'll give it a try anyhow."

Croc backed his Land Rover down nearer the edge of the water. He opened the back gate of it now and pulled out something that looked like a kite. He threw that in the boat along with a couple of long hanks of braided yellow nylon rope and a thing that kinda resembled a big bird if ya sorta squinted at it. Last he pulled out a 12 gauge pump shotgun like you see in the movies. He climbed in with us and we headed out into the lake. Three big men was a pretty heavy load for the john boat so we were riding a little low in the water, but I didn't worry too much about it.

I sat down at the back to handle the motor. Dave sat his considerable bulk up toward the bow and Croc sat in the middle seat facing backward. "Open it up as hard as it'll go, G," he said. "Gotta stir up enough wind to get the kite up." So I cranked the hand throttle all the way up and the little Evinrude started screaming. The wind had come up a little and we were mostly heading into it, so the kite got plenty of lift when Croc held it up and began letting the line slip through his fingers. When the kite was up maybe fifty feet, the lure was hanging and swooping like that gull had, hung and swooped a couple hours before.

"Hey Croc," Dave asked. "That was a damn big fish. How we gonna get it back to shore if it decides to bite?" He had no more than gotten the question out than that fish, if that's what it was, came leaping out of the water and tried to grab the bird lure. It missed. The lure was just a little higher than the leap, so the fish passed under it and landed close to the stern of the boat with a huge splash that washed chilly Pyramid Lake water over us. I cut back on the motor speed and looked at Dave and at Croc awaiting further instruction, but old fish face he didn't have to wait, he dipped down and turned around and came leaping up at the lure a second time. This time the slightly slower speed of the boat and a little bit of lift from his fishy wings did the job wonderfully, and he swallowed that fake bird right down to his tail, then hit the water once more with another huge splash. He jerked the kite right out of the sky.

Croc leaned his full weight back on the nylon line and hollered, "Dave, give me a hand. We need to set the hook better."

Dave jumped up and grabbed a handful of line and the two of them leaned back, pulling the line tight.

Apparently the fish hardly knew he was hooked until both Dave and Croc pulled. The hook set solid, and the fish took off away from the boat. It was pulling against the little motor and the motor was screaming. I reached up and flipped the gear shift into neutral and cranked the throttle down to idle. The fish was running for the middle of the lake and dragging us along like a boat pulling water skiers. It was like something out of Moby Dick with the fish dragging us along at ever increasing speed.

"G," Dave shouted. "Come help!"

I jumped up and grabbed onto the line too, and put my back into trying to hold that fish.

Almost as suddenly as the run had begun it stopped. The line went slack and we began pulling it in and piling it in the bottom of the boat. We were still drifting along with residual motion from our earlier ride but we were losing it fast. The line seemed to be coming in faster than the motion of the boat would account for and in a second, I saw why. The fish was swimming back toward us and when he got close, he made another leap, only he clearly wasn't jumping for any lure. He intended to leap up and attack his tormentors, which meant us. He misjudged his leap just a bit and only his tail slapped us as he went over. The swat knocked us all down, but Dave and Croc were still hanging onto the line.

I decided I wasn't gonna let any fish beat me down without a fight and I grabbed one of the oars. The fish turned and headed back at us again. His aim was better with this leap. He landed at an angle right on top of the boat with a crunch, pinning both Dave and Croc beneath him. I barely had a place to stand but I swung my oar down as hard as I could and connected solidly, then brought it up and hit the fish again.

It is a real testament to how well built that aluminum john boat was that we didn't sink with all the weight of fish and men, and a testament to how strong Big Dave really was that even with this huge flapping fish laying on him, he managed to heave it up enough to reach Croc's shotgun. He jacked a shell into the chamber and fired point blank into that fish's belly then jacked another into it and fired again. The shots blew fish guts and ick all over us, but the fish quite flapping.

I threw down my oar and moved forward hollering, "Dave, you okay? Croc?"

"I'm okay, G, just squished. Help me move this thing off me."

I bent down as much as I could and tried to get a hold on the fish, but it was slimy and there was nothing to grab onto. I turned and picked up my oar again then stuck it under the fish and used it as a lever to lift. Dave was shoving from below and between us, we lifted the thing enough for Dave to scoot out from under it. All that moving and shifting and levering didn't do a thing for the balance of the already tippy boat and the port gunwale went under water a little bit. It scooped a gallon or two of the lake into the boat, but Dave shifted his weight and brought the boat back to center keel, albeit a bit lower in the water.

We hadn't heard anything from Croc. He was face down under the fish more than Dave had been, and I was afraid he was really hurt. The dipped in water was lapping around him and it crossed my mind that a man can drown in a couple of inches of water.

Dave and I tried to move the fish but had the same trouble as before, too slimy and slick, so we picked up both oars and began to lever the fish up. Croc wasn't conscious so he couldn't help by pulling himself out once the weight was up off of him.

"Keep lifting, G," Dave said. "We'll just roll this beast off into the lake."

We put the heave ho into it and sorta slid the slimy beast over the starboard gunwale and back in the water. When the weight shifted again, we dipped another couple of gallons of lake into the boat but all in all the boat floated a good bit higher with the weight of the fish off it. The monster started sinking and pulling the yellow nylon line after it the instant it was completely in the water. Dave grabbed the line and leaned back on it, then quickly flipped a bight of it around his back and over his shoulder.

I jumped over to try to help, but he said, "Check Croc. I got this for now."

Croc was sorta crunched up between the bench seats of the boat, and I'd guess that was what saved his life. Both his and Dave's, because if the full weight of the fish falling from ten feet up had hit them, they would have at least had broken ribs and maybe worse. I squatted down as best I could and noted Croc's mouth and nose were out of the water lapping in the bottom of the boat and he was breathing. I didn't try to straighten him out for fear he had broken bones or internal injuries I might make it worse if I moved him, but I did gently slap his face and say, "Croc, you okay. Wake up now. Come on, wakee wakee."

He groaned and his eyelids fluttered.

"G, I'm not gonna be able to hold on much longer. This is one heavy son of a bitch. Start us toward shore."

"Okay," I answered and turned to the Evinrude. Somewhere in all the splashing and dragging and rocking the engine had quit running. I checked the settings…throttle in start position, gear shift in neutral, tank flow open…and gave the start rope a yank. It coughed and pumped out blue smoke but didn't catch. *Oh Lord,* I thought, worrying and praying all at the same time. *Please, let this damn thing start.* I gave it another hard pull, remembering what the old man had said about flooding it. Once more it coughed and belched a cloud of blue smoke, but then it chugged and chugged again and caught. The revs came up and I sat down, weak in the knees from effort and from relief. I brought the rev's down and slipped the little motor into gear, aiming us at the shore. The boat was heeled over to starboard with the weight of the fish still on the line, and we were taking a little water with the little waves of the lake.

I moved up to try to help Dave but he said, "I got it, G. Bail some of this water out."

I looked around, but there was no bucket or coffee can to be found so I began dipping the water out with my cupped hands. It was slow going and the old saw about trying to hold back the tide with a spoon crossed my mind, but I gained on it enough that we didn't founder.

Dave was showing the strain of the fish's weight and the friction of pulling all that weight through the water. His face was red and his arm and back muscles were quivering with stress. Now, I knew how strong Dave was. I had once seen him pick up and throw a small Honda motorcycle over a considerable distance, and once been physically lifted and carried by those thick steel arms, but those were short bursts of strength, not sustained strain. "You okay, Dave?"

"Yeah," he grunted, clearly having no strength left over for conversation, so I took him at his word and kept dipping water back into the lake.

When I got enough gone I couldn't easily dip more, I turned and reached my long arms around Dave's shoulders like in a bear hug and took hold of the taut line. I don't know how much I helped, but Dave quit shaking quite as much. Then we sat listening to the little Evinrude strain.

Five minutes, or maybe five hundred hours later the john boat scraped bottom and stopped. I let go of Dave and the rope, and rolled out into knee deep water to pull the boat up a little farther then turned back to the line still stretching back into the water. "Okay, I got it Dave, come on out." He let go his hold on the line and the full weight settled on me. The line stripped through my hands for a few inches then stopped as the weight of the fish hit the bottom.

Croc groaned louder than before then said, "Shit! What happened?" He sat up.

Dave, grinning like a wolf about to bite a lamb, said, "Nice of ya to wake up in time to finish landing this thing, Croc."

"You okay?" I asked. "Anything broken?"

He paused a moment, obviously taking inventory, before saying, "Naw. I seem to be more or less together."

"Well then get out of there and help us pull this beast up where we can really get a look at it," Dave said.

The Australian pushed up and stepped over the gunwale into the water then sloshed up to us. "What happened? I don't remember anything after seeing that fish flying toward us."

"Tell ya later," I said. "For now shut up and pull."

He grabbed hold of the line, and we put our backs into it slowly pulling the bulk of the monster to us a few inches at a time. At last we had it more out of the water than in and quit pulling.

Dave was shaking his head looking at this thing. "What hath God Wrought?" he said.

"I think I asked before, Croc, but how the hell are we gonna get this thing out of here and down to La Jolla to Scripps?"

"No worries," he said and pulled his cell phone out of his pocket. He handed it to me. "But first I want you to take a picture."

He waded back into the water and assumed the big game hunter pose with his hand on the fish. With his other hand, he waved away some flies that had suddenly gathered around him and the fish. "Hurry up," he said.

I got the phone up and aimed as he flapped around chasing the flies, and then he was gone. Croc and fish were just gone. The beat up john boat and the lake and a few of the flies were still there, but Croc and the fish were gone.

"What the hell?"

"Did you get the picture?" Dave asked.

I looked at the screen of the phone, but there was nothing there.

"Damn!"

"Fisherman's luck, Dave. Just like my old man said. Wet ass and hungry guts."

THE END

ACKNOWLEDGEMENTS

"TIBURCIO'S TREASURE"
First published in Antelope Valley Anthology II
"Red Skies like nowhere else on Earth"
October, 2006

"WINDS OF THE GREAT MOJAVE"
first published in
Antelope Valley Anthology III
"Aldous Huxley Slept Here"
October, 2007

"SLEEPING BEAUTY"
first published in
"Pump up the Purse"
Canadian Fiction
March, 2009

"ILLEGAL ALIENS"
First published in
Aliens Among Us Anthology
Metahuman Press
February, 2012

VISIT OUR WEBSITE
FOR THE FULL INVENTORY
OF QUALITY BOOKS:

http://www.roguephoenixpress.com

Representing Excellence in Publishing

Quality trade paperbacks and downloads

in multiple formats,

in genres ranging from historical to contemporary romance, mystery and science fiction.

Visit the website then bookmark it.

We add new titles each month!

www.ingramcontent.com/pod-product-compliance
Lightning Source LLC
Chambersburg PA
CBHW072032170626
46811CB00008B/3042